HILL OF DARKNESS

Hill of Darkness

JAN MICHAEL

ff

faber and faber

For Jessica and Elisabeth

First published in Great Britain in 1995
by Faber and Faber Limited
3 Queen Square London WC1N 3AU

Photoset by Keyboard Services, Luton
Printed in England by Clays Ltd, St Ives plc

A CIP record of this book
is available from the British Library

ISBN 0–571–17407–8

2 4 6 8 10 9 7 5 3 1

CHAPTER 1

Left foot, right, one foot then another, silently, cautiously, left foot—

It was hot and dark under the trees where the leaves above Julia's head shut out the tropical moonlight. She could not see. She blundered into something light and soft and sticky. She reached up and tried to wipe it off her forehead. It stuck to her fingers. She tried again and it clung to her hair. She tore at it then with both hands; she rolled the sticky stuff into a ball and threw it to the ground in disgust. Don't be silly, Julia, she said to herself, it's only a cobweb. That didn't help. She thought of the huge furry spider that would be hiding somewhere in the far corner of the large web, watching her, and she shuddered.

Walk on, she told herself.

One step upwards, climbing, then another, and another—

Cackling. Something cackled, loudly, just to the right of her.

Julia swayed in fright. Losing her balance, she began to topple. She put out her hand for support and touched warm skin where she had expected tree. There was another cackle a little further off now.

Under her fingers she could feel Thomas's pulse beating as hard as her own. 'It's only a bird,' her older brother said, his voice trembling a little. 'You can let go of me now,' and he shook her off.

Silently her lips formed 'I hate you,' but she knew she didn't, not really. She would never have dared set foot on this hill without him, not even in daylight. She brushed the sweat from her forehead and flapped her short nightgown, fanning her body.

'It's your turn to lead,' she said, but Thomas had already left her side. She dropped to the ground on hands and knees. It might be safer that way. She followed the whisper of leaves in Thomas's wake. She had dared him to come up The Hill, as they called it, never expecting him to take her on. But he had. She had waited for her parents to go to bed and waited longer till she judged they had fallen asleep and then she had gone in and shaken him awake. And now here they were, on the greegree man's territory where no child should ever come. Something had drawn her to it, to that dark scar in the side of The Hill, now not so far away. She was terrified yet she had to go on.

Right hand, left knee, left hand, right knee, mouth dry, easing aside branches, shaking beetles from her hands. She was all alone in the world, far from home and bed, far from the sea and its comforting sighing, far from her parents and Thérèse and –

Where was Thomas?

She stopped and listened. She got to her feet and peered in front of her in the darkness.

Nothing. Her scalp crawled.

'Thomas!' she hissed, concentrating all her mind on him. She didn't want to be alone, not up here.

'Thomas!' more loudly. A sob escaped her. What if, because of her, what if the greegree man had taken Thomas and was this minute tying him up, sharpening his knife, and setting his pots ready?

It was so still!

'Thomas!' She forced herself up through the trees, not caring now how much noise she made. 'Thomas! Where are you?' she cried.

A branch whipped at her cheek, scratching her. Tears gathered in her eyes. One trickled down on to her lips. She licked it in, tasting the salt. Perhaps the greegree man collected tears too.

Suddenly, in front of her, the trees gave way on to a clearing where the moonlight poured and she saw Thomas, lit up, sitting with his back to her, his head down and his arms around his knees, curled in a tight ball. She stumbled over and squatted beside him. 'Thomas?'

He lifted his head and stared blankly at her. 'Listen, Julia. Don't move,' he whispered out of the corner of his mouth.

She froze, allowing only her eyes to roam. Above her loomed the narrow peak of The Hill, black and ghastly. She and Thomas were dreadfully exposed in the silver moonlight. Anyone or anything out there could see them. The silence swelled. Ahead of her the trees formed a solid, dark wall. She scanned them in dread. She stared until her eyes hurt. A branch broke. Something in the black mass wavered. A shape seemed slowly to detach itself from the surrounding darkness. It took a step forward into the clearing towards them.

She shuddered and jumped to her feet in an instant. 'Run, Thomas! Run!' and she turned and plunged back into the blackness that closed in behind her, running as best she could, not caring what she trod under her bare feet, not scared of the trees and spiders' webs any more for at least they were trees and webs and not that shape that had started to come for them and was chasing them now, oh –

'Holy Mary, Mother of God, pray for us sinners now and at the hour of our death, Holy Mary, Mother of God, pray for us –' over and over again, she chanted. Something was crashing down the hill behind her but she did not stop to see if it was Thomas, turned so silent and strange, or the greegree man. On she ran, tripping and stumbling down The Hill till at last she could see the tops of the coconut trees ahead of her, on and on down until she was on the grassy plain beneath those palms. She threw herself down on her tummy, catching her breath, and there was Thomas, mercifully, at her side, retching, gasping, 'Don't stop! Come on!'

But she had rolled over and was gazing up at the moon, now once more her friend. The coconut trees stood straight and tall like sentinels, guarding them.

'It's all right,' she said, 'he won't come after us here. We're safe. He never leaves The Hill.'

'Who says?'

'Thérèse says.'

A coconut thumped loudly to the ground ahead of them.

'I want to go home,' Thomas said.

They crossed the plain beneath the tall trees, going the long way round so that they would not have to pass the stone punishment cells where slaves had been chained to rings in the walls. The walls should have been overgrown years ago but someone kept the vegetation cut back and the great iron rings remained there, rusting, a reminder of man's cruelty to man, their father said.

Gusts of wind lifted their hair from their faces and set the palm leaves rattling. On the way to The Hill, Julia had thought the rattling sounded like knives being sharpened. Now it was reassuring. Cicadas kept up a constant high chirruping and jangling all around, frogs croaked and sang.

Once across the plain they turned inland again up a sandy drive and took a short cut through the bushes. When they reached the stone bungalow that was home, they avoided the squeaking French windows and squeezed noiselessly through the ornate ironwork that ran almost down the length of the sitting room.

'Good-night,' they whispered, 'good-night.'

Julia tiptoed past her parents' open door. They had not stirred when she and Thomas had left the house and they did not stir now. She went into her own room and stood at the window, looking up at The Hill. She didn't know what she expected to see. But if, she thought, if the greegree man was looking down now from his hiding place, would he be able to see her in her bed? There was no glass, there were no curtains or shutters to stop him looking in. She felt small and exposed.

Her bed stood halfway along the wall, jutting out into the middle of the room. She moved it towards the window, lifting it as quietly as she could, one corner at a time. Fortunately the wood was light and so was the coconut-hair mattress and it didn't take her long. She lay down on it to try it out. The window was above her now and she could no longer see The Hill. She got back into bed, pulling the sheet high over her head to keep her safe.

She couldn't sleep. Never before the silence of The Hill, had she noticed the noises of the night. She did now. She pulled back the sheet and listened, separating them. The clock ticking from the hallway outside her room, the cicadas sawing away outside, dogs barking, somewhere further away the sound of a cock crowing. In the moonlight she could see the lizards running across the ceiling above her head, dark shapes on the paler plaster. One of them darted across to a corner. From another corner she heard the faintest plop as one of them fell, dead, to the floor. The sounds were the sounds of all nights. She pulled the sheet back over her head. Her eyelids grew heavier, her leg twitched. She slept.

CHAPTER 2

In the morning, a macaw croaking loudly on the grass outside woke Julia. She knelt on the bed, about to go out through the window as she usually did, but thought better of it. The Hill was out there. She turned her back on it and walked slowly and deliberately towards the door, the hairs at the back of her neck prickling. Once she was out of the room, she went more quickly through the hall to Thomas's bedroom. Its windows were on the other side, overlooking the harbour. Early morning sunshine was pouring in.

She sat on his bed and tried to tweak the sheet from his clenched fist. He groaned and grasped it more tightly.

'It's *me*,' she said, leaning forward. 'Julia.'

His fingers relaxed and he opened one eye.

'I took ages to get to sleep,' she told him. 'Did you?'

He grunted and closed his eye again.

'Thomas.' She shook his shoulder gently.

He didn't respond.

She tugged at the sheet, harder. 'Do you think the greegree man really saw us?' she asked.

No reaction.

'Thomas?' She waited, trying to be patient. She urgently wanted to know.

7

At last Thomas turned on to his back and looked properly at her. He seemed to be thinking.

'I suppose I do,' he said finally. 'Yes.'

Her tummy went cold.

But then he frowned. 'Oh, I don't know.'

'Which?' she asked carefully. 'You suppose so or you don't know?' She sat absolutely still, careful not to jiggle. It was vital that she found out. She got impatient of waiting. 'If he did see us, do you think he'll come after us?' she prompted.

His eyes closed again.

'You don't want to think about it,' she challenged him.

They flew open. 'You were the one who said he never leaves The Hill,' he retorted.

'Yes. Well. That's what Thérèse said,' she answered a little uncertainly, wondering if she'd perhaps imagined it. Her hand strayed up to a mosquito bite and began to scratch.

'So go and ask Thérèse,' he said, turning over.

She stopped scratching. 'But–'

He was pummelling his pillow into shape beneath his head and curling up again. Her voice trailed away.

She found it again. 'You're scared,' she accused, trying to stir him that way.

'I'm not,' he muttered.

'I don't believe you.'

He pulled the sheet over his head. 'Go away,' he said in a muffled voice. 'Leave me alone. Want to go back to sleep.'

'Well I'm scared too.' She waited, hoping he'd

8

change his mind and go on talking to her. But he had closed down the way he sometimes did when he didn't want to discuss things.

In that case she would go and find Thérèse. She climbed on to Thomas's window sill, jumped down on the grass the other side and ran the length of the bungalow to where Thérèse slept. She was already dressed, sitting on her bed and plaiting her hair.

Julia watched her from the doorway. 'Can I do that?'

'Not this morning.' Thérèse's fingers deftly wound strands of springy hair around each other, thin brown fingers twining in and out. She didn't look up.

Julia went and stood close, breathing in the smell of the coconut oil that Thérèse rubbed into her hair.

'Oh please.' She spoke in Creole, the island language. She used it with almost everyone except her parents and sometimes Thomas.

'*Non*. No, I'm late. I have to get your breakfast. Where have you been? Your legs are full of scratches.'

Julia looked down and saw long pink lines, some with little crusts of blood, covering her shins and knees. 'We went for a walk,' she said.

'At *night*?' Thérèse asked.

Julia nodded. 'And Thomas says I'm to ask you if the greegree man will come after us.'

Thérèse's fingers paused in their plaiting.

'We went up The Hill,' Julia explained, boasting. 'And he may have s – Oh!' She broke off. Too late, she realized she had made a mistake. She should never have told Thérèse.

9

Thérèse's head jerked up. 'Where did you say you went?' Her voice was quiet, very quiet, and there was no smile in her eyes.

'The Hill,' Julia whispered.

They stared at each other. The sharp tapping of shoes came through to them from the dining room. Quickly Thérèse coiled her plaits to the top of her head and fixed them with two curved pins, not once moving her eyes off Julia. 'I told you never to go there.'

'I know. But – but Thomas and I want to know, if the greegree man saw us, will he come after us?'

Thérèse froze. She gazed at Julia, and her gaze made Julia uneasy. In a way Thérèse didn't seem to be looking at her at all.

Julia shifted from one foot to the other. She looked away from Thérèse and concentrated hard on a shaft of sunlight that had just reached the bed and was coming in through the high window like the beam from a torch.

A bell tinkled from the dining room.

'*Allez.*' Thérèse pushed Julia away. 'Your mother is ringing for breakfast and I have not yet finished making it. We'll talk about this later.'

Julia went into the dining room.

Her mother looked up, grey eyes in a tanned face. She held out a slim arm with thin gold bangles hanging from it.

Julia went over and nestled against her. 'Hello,' she said.

Her mother pushed Julia's fringe off her face. 'Hello, darling. Have you been up long?'

Julia shook her head and cuddled in closer, glad to feel the safety of her mother's warmth. Her father came in, dark from the sun and sturdy looking in his tropical kit of open-necked shirt, shorts, knee-length socks and lace-up shoes, all in white. There was a tetchy expression on his face. 'Have you seen my pen, Elizabeth?'

'No,' Julia's mother answered.

'Are you sure you haven't moved it?'

Julia went over to greet him, ignoring the conversation, and lifted her face to be kissed. 'Hello, my poppet,' he said, dark, deep-set eyes smiling at her. 'Where's Thomas?'

'He's still in bed,' she told him.

'I expect your pen's where you left it, darling,' her mother answered her father as she turned a page of the journal in front of her, picked up a spoon and began to eat her paw paw.

'I'll go and get him,' Julia offered.

She did, rousing him more noisily this time. 'Breakfast's ready. You're to get up.'

She drew back and watched Thomas crawl drowsily out of bed. 'I asked Thérèse. She didn't actually answer.'

He stood up quickly. 'You did what?' he asked.

'I asked Thérèse,' she said again. 'You told me to,' she added defensively.

'You idiot! I didn't mean it.'

She stared miserably at him. 'Then why did you tell me to?'

'Because I wanted to sleep. Because I – Oh, what a stupid thing to do!'

He pulled off his T-shirt. 'Did Thérèse really not answer?' he asked her more calmly.

'Not really,' Julia said, thinking hard. 'She went a bit funny. She kind of – stared at me.'

Thomas stepped into his shorts and put on a shirt. 'I think,' he said at length, doing up the buttons, 'I think we should just forget what we did.'

'How?' she asked.

'By forgetting, that's how.'

'Why?' she asked.

'Well have you got a better suggestion?'

She considered. 'No,' she said. 'Not at the moment,' she added, just to be on the safe side.

'Right then. Today is Saturday,' he told her.

'I know that,' she said scornfully.

'No, listen. Today's Saturday,' he repeated. 'And it's going to be like any other Saturday. We've done what we did and it's over now. Let's forget it,' he said firmly. 'That's what I think.'

He made it sound convincing, and that persuaded her. Fine, she thought, then she would let today be like any other Saturday.

She considered for a moment then went back to the table as Thomas headed for the lavatory. Her parents had almost finished their fruit.

'He's coming,' she said, sitting down and sliding in her chair, relishing the scraping noise it made on the cement floor and the way it made her parents wince. On Saturdays she was allowed to have breakfast in her

12

nightgown and not her school uniform, her navy blue pleated tunic with a belt over it and a white blouse under, a straw hat and sandals. Her nightie was much more comfortable.

'There's a ship due in next week. Might have some post from home,' her father told her, 'and potatoes.' She sighed loudly and squeezed lime over her paw paw. Her father adored potatoes but they didn't grow here in the tropics. Julia was perfectly happy with yams, rice and sweet potatoes. And her parents always called Britain home. She and Thomas never did. Home was where they lived, here in the Seychelles on the main island Mahé, not that other place of grey skies and washed-out people trudging along dirty pavements in the drizzle.

'I want you to go with Thérèse this morning and have your hair cut, darling,' Julia's mother said. That meant it would end up only a little longer than a boy's. Julia didn't mind. Her mother's hair fell softly to her shoulders in light brown curls. 'And ask him to take a lot off,' she said to Thérèse.

'Yes, Madame.' Thérèse took away Julia's plate and brought her some toast.

Julia tried to catch her eye but couldn't. She dipped her knife into the jam. 'Please may I have some curtains in my bedroom?' she asked, spreading jam carefully into every corner of her toast.

Her mother looked at her, surprised. 'You always said you didn't want any.'

'I do now. Marie's got curtains,' she added.

'Oh well, that settles it,' her mother teased. 'I've

13

got some pretty yellow cotton you'd probably like. Perhaps Thérèse wouldn't mind making them up for you tonight?' She looked questioningly at Thérèse.

'No, this afternoon,' Julia said insistently and rather rudely.

A glance passed between her mother and Thérèse. Thérèse shrugged slightly. Then she looked at Julia, long and thoughtfully. Julia felt herself begin to blush. Thérèse, she realized, knew why she wanted the curtains, knew why she wanted her windows covered. Her eyes dropped.

'We'll see,' her mother said. 'And only if Thérèse has the time,' she went on.

Wisely, Julia left it at that. She had learned it was best not to pester her mother.

'May I leave the table?' she asked.

Her mother raised her curved eyebrows at her. 'You haven't eaten your toast yet.'

'I want to take it with me.'

'Julia – ,' warningly.

'To my tree,' she added quickly. 'It's Saturday, Mummy,' she pleaded. Saturday like any other Saturday, she reminded herself.

'All right. Leave it here till you get your book. I don't want your crumbs all over the place, encouraging cockroaches.'

'OK.' Julia ran to her room and picked up *Alice Through the Looking Glass*, sent out on the last ship by her uncle. Once when they were in Britain on leave she had heard him tell her mother that he would send books regularly so that they would not

14

feel cut off. Cut off from what? she always wondered.

She skittered back to the table.

'We'll be back from the office about half past twelve. All right? Julia –' her mother had just spotted her legs. 'What are those scratches?'

Julia paused, toast in hand, and looked guiltily at her mother. Thomas, just sitting down, dropped his knife on the floor and when she turned to look he stared a warning at her. She shook her head almost imperceptibly; of course she wouldn't tell her parents. 'Oh they're nothing,' she answered and was out of the dining room before there were any more questions and across the grass to where the low guava tree grew crookedly at the edge of the terraces. In three swings she was up in her favourite spot, her 'armchair', two branches strategically placed, one under her thighs, another at her back, ripe green guavas for the picking all around. She took a bite of toast, opened her book and began to read. She read slowly at first and then avidly as she imagined herself stepping through the mirror into the mysterious world on the other side.

She didn't hear Simba their ancient mongrel barking at the departure of her parents as he tried to chase their car down the drive, didn't notice the sounds of the bugle as Thomas signalled through the trees to his friend Marcel that he was going over to play, didn't hear Thérèse calling her to go and get dressed.

'Get dressed, I said!'

She heard now; Thérèse was standing at the bottom

of her tree, and she was surprised at the cross note in Thérèse's voice.

'And hurry up.'

Startled, Julia slid to the ground. She opened her mouth to speak but thought better of it and went meekly to her room to wash and dress. When she came out, Thérèse was waiting for her, baskets in hand.

'Where are your shoes?'

'I don't need them. It's Saturday.'

'You do need them. We're going into town. Go on, go and put them on.'

Julia went back for her sandals, sat on the floor and buckled the hard leather to her feet. She knew better than to argue with Thérèse when she was cross.

CHAPTER 3

They took the path into town, not the road, entering it where exposed red clay damp from the night's moisture gave off a deep earthy smell, and still Thérèse didn't speak. Shafts of sunlight came down through the leaves on to the path, making whirly patterns of the dust kicked up by the scratching chickens. 'As many chickens as people on this island,' her father often said, swerving the car to avoid running them over. Julia did not know how people knew which chickens were whose. She started humming, a Creole song that Thérèse had taught her only the week before, about coconut love:

> 'A-io, chérie, comme père pas là,
> a nous faire nous l'amour coco.
> A-io, chérie, comme père pas là – ow, that hurt.'

Thérèse had hold of her hand and was tugging. 'Don't dawdle. We haven't time this morning.'
'Why are you so cross?'
'Why do you think?'
'Oh.' Julia had succeeded in blanking it out. Saturday, her book, and now that the sun was shining and the path familiar, the night somehow seemed a long time ago.

'Don't try and smile at me,' Thérèse said. 'It'll make no difference.' She stopped and faced Julia, put her hands on Julia's shoulders and gave her a shake. 'It's dangerous up that hill. You knew that. The greegree man *eats* children like you.'

Julia stared at her.

'All right,' Thérèse relented. 'I don't know that he eats them. But he does melt children's fat down into candles.'

'I'm not fat,' Julia protested.

'No, you're not,' Thérèse agreed. 'But he would find fat on you. Once, when I was little –' She broke off suddenly.

'Go on. Thérèse? Go on.'

'No. You have to have your hair cut and I promised Noellie I'd get vegetables for her, and I want to speak to –. There's no time for stories now.'

Julia watched Thérèse bend to pick up the baskets she had put on the ground. She hesitated and straightened, facing Julia again, not touching. She gazed intently at her and Julia gazed back.

'Listen,' she said. The sharp note in her voice had gone. Now she sounded grave and solemn.

'Yes?' Julia stood quite still.

'Never tell anyone what you did last night. Not your parents, not your friends, not even Marie.'

Their eyes were locked. 'All right,' said Julia.

'*Promise*.'

'I promise.'

Thérèse picked up the baskets. She held one out to Julia to carry and Julia took it, the action sealing the promise. Julia felt a great sense of relief.

Thérèse bent and kissed her on the forehead. '*Bien*,' she said, 'good.'

After that, Thérèse walked a bit more slowly and when they reached the small wooden hut where the old man squatted, deftly carving coconut shells into pots for the American tourists who came on cruise ships twice a year, she even stopped to talk. He was a distant cousin of hers.

'Julia-O!'

Julia looked round and saw Cécile, a girl from her class, waving her over. She put down the pot she had been fingering, left Thérèse's side and followed Cécile up the wooden stairs to her small house, feeling clumsy as she often did with her islander classmates who were a good head shorter than she was. Cécile's legs were firm and round too, unlike Julia's skinny matchsticks. She envied Cécile her hair as well. Her own was straight and white from the sun whereas everyone else at school had black hair of all sorts, long, thick and glossy, short and head-hugging, friz-zily plaited. Cécile's was tight against her head and crinkly.

A baby was crying inside. Julia followed Cécile into the room where she slept with her brothers and sisters and parents. Every inch of the walls had bright pic-tures from magazines cut out and pasted over it. Last time Julia had come, except for a wooden crucifix, the walls had been bare.

'Oh,' she gasped, stunned by so many images, not knowing which one to go and look at first.

Cécile was pleased at her reaction. 'We all chose the pictures and Mum and I stuck them up. Aren't they beautiful?'

'Yes,' said Julia with feeling, her eyes flitting from a picture of the Queen and royal family to one of a gorgeous model with long hair sitting in a moss-covered valley to one of a gleaming Rolls-Royce parked outside a castle.

A toddler who had been playing with the baby came over, chortling, claiming her attention. She looked away from the pictures and swung him on her hip as she had seen others do, while Cécile picked the baby up from the cot. Julia nuzzled his sticky neck and wished she had lots of smaller brothers and sisters, instead of being just the younger of two. The toddler squirmed and demanded to be put down.

'Let's see if Papa will give us some honey,' Cécile said, and out they went again with the baby, down the steps and round to the back of the house where Cécile's father was taking a honeycomb from the tree. He and Julia exchanged shy greetings and he passed her a piece dripping with honey. There were bits of insects in the comb, a couple of legs here, a head there, and a dead bee in one corner. She hesitated.

'Eat it. It's all right. The bee too.' He laughed as she crunched into the corner of the comb. She had not meant to eat the bee but the cloying honey and squishy wax were so delicious that she forgot where it was and realized, too late, that it must have gone down inside her.

She passed the comb to Cécile who bit into it as they walked round to the front of the house again. 'Can you come to the market?' she asked her as she heard Thérèse calling.

Cécile shook her head. Her dark eyes flashed. 'I have to look after the little ones.'

Thérèse called again.

Quickly Julia took a last bite of the comb and passed it back once more to Cécile, getting her fingers caught in the stuff. They glued stickily together.

'Julia-O!'

'Bye, Cécile.' Quickly she joined Thérèse, trying to rub the stuff from her fingers as they carried on down the path, but the stickiness reminded her of something. Cobwebs, spiders, The Hill at night. She stopped and looked down at her fingers. Don't be silly, she thought to herself, it's only honey. She put her fingers to her mouth and sucked them clean, one by one, and ran after Thérèse again.

The path came out in front of the big cathedral. Two towers reached to the sky, each with a clock on it. One said nine thirty, the other one o'clock. One was wrong, to confuse the Devil. Shallow stone steps the width of the building led up to the door. Thérèse hesitated, then seemed to make up her mind and headed for the steps. Julia went willingly with her. She loved the contrast of the cool, dark interior with the heat and brightness outside; it always made her dreamy. Some light filtered through the stained-glass windows set high in the walls. The rest came only from a bank of candles flickering before a side altar. Thérèse genuflected at the door and made the sign of the cross. Julia copied her and followed her over to the candles. Thérèse dropped some cents into a box, took a fresh white candle and lit it, her lips moving in silent prayer.

'Who did you light the candle for?' Julia asked when she saw that her lips had stopped moving.

'My father.'

'Oh.' Thérèse's father had been killed only the month before, falling from the open back of one of the lorries that served as the island's buses. They had benches down both sides and standing room in between if you were clever enough to keep your balance. The driver had taken a corner too fast, the lorry had swayed and Thérèse's father had fallen into the cloud of dust thrown up by the thick tyres.

'Do you want to light one? Here.' Thérèse gave her a couple of cents.

'I don't know who to light it for.'

'Light it for someone who's died.'

But Julia didn't know anyone who was dead, only Thérèse's father and she'd never actually met him.

'Someone who's ill then.'

Julia didn't know anyone who was ill either.

'Then just light it for your mother and father.'

Julia dropped the cents in the wooden box, took one of the slender candles and dipped the wick carefully into the candle Thérèse had just lit. Behind the candles, Jesus and Mary watched her patiently. The painting was bigger than the altar and the figures seemed huge. Julia fitted the burning candle into one of the candle-holders and the flame shone out straight and true. Her eyes followed the thin plume of smoke trying to reach the ceiling of the cathedral.

Julia sniffed her fingers as they emerged into the sunlight outside. They smelled of candle and church.

'Were those candles made of children's fat?' she asked Thérèse suddenly.

'No!'

Thérèse looked so shocked Julia wished she hadn't asked. She hadn't really thought they were made with children's fat. She had just wanted to make sure.

'What are they made of?'

'I don't know. It's time we had your hair cut.' Thérèse was getting cross again.

CHAPTER 4

Market Street, the busiest part of the small town, was very close. Women and men with baskets of fish and fruit on their heads were jostled by rickshaws; cars honked their way through shouting traders. Thérèse and Julia dodged from one stall to another.

They stopped halfway down where a cluster of black umbrellas hoisted on poles gave shade to the chair beneath. The man squatting beside it, smoking, stood up when he saw them stop. While he and Thérèse agreed on a price, Julia got into the chair, tilting her head back to look at the underside of the umbrellas, at the way they overlapped like the scales of a pineapple.

She bent her head for the barber to fasten the nylon cape round her neck. She traced the blue dots and lines on it till they dazzled her, while all around the stallholders sang their praises of their fish and yams, mangos and tomatoes. The barber cut, and her hair fell down like feathers till it would be as short as a boy's again.

'You have a lot of scratches on your legs,' the barber said.

'Yes,' Julia answered and crossed them quickly. She wished everyone would stop telling her about the scratches. She thought she heard whispering behind

24

her. Was it Thérèse? She could not turn her head to check because the barber held it firmly when she tried, as if he didn't want her to look. Anyway, it couldn't have been Thérèse, she reasoned; Thérèse had said she was leaving her there while she got the vegetables. The barber pushed her head to one side. Was he cross with her too, because of the scratches? Might Thérèse have told him? Surely not, she thought. Surely the promise not to tell applied to them both.

By the time Julia's hair was cut and she had found Thérèse, bargaining not for vegetables but for a length of printed cotton – 'for a wedding I'm going to next week,' Thérèse said – she had decided she would go to her parents' office and play there. When she asked, Thérèse nodded and said that was fine.

It was only about ten minutes' walk from the market to the office, along the only stretch of tarmacked road on the island. Wooden houses with balconies and gardens lined one side. On the other was the sea and an earthen pavement under the trees. Julia reached the pavement and looked round, just in case Thérèse was watching her, but she wasn't, so she unbuckled her sandals and took them off. The baked earth of the pavement was warm and she slid the soles of her feet along it as she walked. In a way she was pleased to be on her own and away from Thérèse.

She stopped and looked out to sea in case Thomas was out there sailing. He and Marcel had a boat of their own which they kept moored at Short Pier. Its distinctive green sail meant that it was easy to spot. Not a sign of it today though.

As Julia turned back, her eyes met those of the leper. She jumped and stepped back. He seemed to have appeared from nowhere. She felt sure she hadn't seen him coming. They had told her that he wasn't a leper any more, that it didn't matter anyway, but she had seen the ruins of an old leper colony on Round Island with its chains and kennel-like cells and was wary. His face frightened her. He had no nose, only two holes in a flat face. '*Bonjour*. Good morning,' she muttered and walked on quickly. She crossed herself when she had gone past as she had once seen Thérèse do. Heart hammering, she broke into a run, then stopped, suddenly ashamed, knowing that her parents would say she was behaving badly.

She climbed the grassy slope to her parents' office, at one end of the long low Department of Education. When she reached the verandah outside their room she sat down, brushed the soles of her feet with her hand, put her sandals neatly beside a pillar and went in. Her parents sat at desks in opposite corners of the room. Seeing the shadow fall into the room, they both paused in their writing.

'That looks better, darling,' her mother said. 'Are you just popping in, or are you waiting for us to go home?'

'Waiting,' Julia answered. 'Thérèse said I could.'

Her father grunted. Julia went and stood in front of his desk, watching his dark stubby hands race across the page, filling it with spidery sloping handwriting. Dark hairs covered the backs of his hands, as curly as those on his legs.

'What are candles made of?' she asked. She could at least find out about that.

'Wax,' he said, his pen still moving over the paper. 'And tallow.' He wrote some more. 'I think,' he added.

'Where does wax come from?'

He paused and looked up, pen poised. 'Bees, from honeycombs.'

Honeycombs, she thought with a start, remembering the delicious stuff, warm and gluey. Gluey as cobwebs.

'Now shoo,' he told her. 'Go upstairs, I've got a lot to do.'

But she stood her ground.

'What's tallow?'

He put down his pen. 'Julia, this is an office. I'm working and so is Mummy. You can stay and wait for us, but only if you're quiet. Go upstairs and look it up. It'll be in the dictionary or the encyclopaedia. Go on now. Shoo.' He began writing again.

Julia went then. She climbed the stairs to the room above, which was used by her mother to lecture groups of teachers brought into the capital from the village schools. It was empty today and hot with the fan off and the doors closed. Julia opened them wide, and then went to the shelves for a dictionary and the one-volume encyclopaedia. She carried the heavy books out on to the rickety balcony at the front and sat down, her back against the warm wooden walls, her legs through the carved balustrade, and sighed contentedly. No one else came up here when her mother wasn't lecturing, none of the office clerks or messengers, nobody. She breathed in the lovely smell of sun on wood, dusty chalk and cinnamon from the tree whose crown was just beneath her feet. The paint was blistered and peeling from the floorboards. Idly she helped it free, humming. It was one of her favourite places on Saturday mornings when she had nothing better to do, waiting for her parents, and by now she had almost cleared the whole corner of paint. The bleached patch showed up bare against the surrounding pale green. She reached the end of the plank and nodded, pleased with herself.

Only now did she turn to the encyclopaedia and look up candles. There was nothing. There was candidiasis and candlemas but no candle in between. She closed it and picked up the dictionary. 'Cylinder of wax, tallow, etc. enclosing wick, for giving light,' it said. Wax she knew about. She turned to the Ts, looking for tallow.

'Substance got by melting animal fat, used for making candles, etc.' Tallow was animal fat. There. It said so, black on white, so it must be true. The words stared up at her from the page. Animals included people, she thought, children. Therefore some candles would indeed be made of children's fat. Not the ones in church, all right, but others could be. Even the dictionary knew that.

A brilliant red cardinal flitted past, distracting her for a moment. The bird circled and landed, chattering at her. She examined it, looking for fat, and carefully reached out a hand, but it darted into the air at the last

28

minute, evading her. Beyond where it had perched, at the bottom of the grass slope where the crimson Flamboyant trees grew, she could see the road. A car drove past, but she didn't recognize it. There were some people walking into town, a rickshaw went past, a bicycle. The road looked the same as it always had – and yet there was something different, as if she was seeing it with other eyes. It was familiar and yet strangely silent and still.

A gaudy caterpillar crawled on to her fingers. It was as long as her hand, green and covered in bright red spots. As it headed for her wrist she shook it off, not wanting it to crawl on up her arm. She wondered which candles burned better, wax or tallow. She would not ask. If she did not ask, she would not have to know. Not knowing would be better, she thought. Besides, she reminded herself firmly, this was a Saturday like any other. The caterpillar crawled across the wooden boards away from her, humping, stretching, slithering, quivering, its hair sticking out like soft bristles.

'Go away!' she said to it, out aloud. It didn't. It froze instead. She got up and scooped it to the edge of the balcony. She was about to throw it over. At the last minute she paused. 'Sorry,' she said to it, 'I'm sorry,' and went inside for a sketch pad and crayons and began drawing it instead.

By the time her mother came to fetch her, the drawing was almost finished.

CHAPTER 5

On the way home, Julia's mother turned left and drew up in front of Marcel's house. Immediately Julia was out of the car and running round to the back where Marcel had his den.

'Marcel! Thomas!' she called. 'We're going to Grand' Anse. We're taking a picnic!'

A dark head looked out of the coconut-matting hut.

'Stop there!' Marcel ordered.

Julia obeyed immediately, putting her feet together and biting her lip. 'Why can't I come in?' she asked.

'Because,' Thomas said, looking out beside Marcel. 'What is it, Julia?'

'We're going to Grand' Anse for a picnic. You're invited too,' she said to Marcel. 'Are you coming?' and she turned and ran into the house, not waiting to see if they would follow her.

Inside her parents were settling into cane chairs, long iced drinks in their hands.

'Julia. Hello.' Mrs Le Geyt had uncoiled to her feet. She was tall and lanky and her long hair was always wound round in plaits close to her head. 'Would you like a lime juice?'

Julia's eyes flickered towards her mother. 'Just one

drink, darling, we won't be long,' she said. 'Did you find the boys?'

Julia nodded, and took the glass Mrs Le Geyt held out to her, smiling back at the gash of red on her thin wide mouth. 'Thank you.' Marcel's mother walked back to her chair, tiptoeing on her bare feet the way she always did, as if she was wearing high heels. Her toenails, painted as brilliantly as her lips, flashed.

'I wish you'd let me borrow her for a week, Elizabeth,' she said to Julia's mother. 'We could swap. You could take Marcel and I'd have Julia.'

'Fine,' her mother answered, laughing but she held out an arm to Julia who pressed into her side nervously while the grown-ups smiled at her. She was relieved when the boys came in and noisily helped themselves to the lime juice on the table, taking the attention away from her.

Julia's father stretched. 'Go and fetch your bathing togs, Marcel, and we'll be off.'

Once home Julia went to the kitchen with her mother to see what there was for a picnic while Marcel and Thomas were sent into the garden with a sharp knife to cut a pineapple and some bananas. The bread Noellie had just baked was cooling on the table. Noellie and her mother began to slice it for sandwiches. Julia idly put her hand on to the bowl, still with traces of flour, balanced on top of the scales, and watched the needle swing round the dial as she pressed. When it reached 4 ounces, long antennae and the head of a cockroach appeared at the edge of the dial, between the numbers and the glass. Julia stared in fascination at the brown antennae. They were as long as her fingers, jointed and hairy. They flickered, first to the left then to the right as more of the cockroach, its wings as shiny as brown metal, edged into sight. Abruptly she lifted her hand. The needle on the dial swung back to zero and the feelers vanished. She began slowly to press it again.

'Don't play with that, Julia,' Noellie warned. 'You might break it.'

Julia looked down at the dial but there was nothing there this time. She released it and pushed the scales away from her.

At the table Noellie was putting sardines inside her pile of sandwiches. She broke off to reach down the front of her dress. From her enormous bra she produced a man's handkerchief and dabbed at the sweat that was trickling down the sides of her face; Julia's mother, cotton dress glued damply to her back, was filling other sandwiches with mashed-up egg and sliced tomato from the garden.

'Are you coming with us, Noellie?' Julia asked, one leg swinging.

'Noellie will be glad to have an afternoon here in peace without you pestering her,' her mother said firmly.

'What about Thérèse?'

'Go and ask her if you want.'

Thérèse was spreading the washing out on the grass and over the red-berried compeche hedge and said she needed the afternoon to make her dress for the wedding. And to make Julia's curtains, she added. Julia grinned. In fact the one time Thérèse had come swimming with them she had kept her dress on and refused to go further out than her knees. She was afraid of the sea. Most islanders were.

Julia wasn't afraid. Grand' Anse was special. Usually they went to Beau Vallon to swim. You could go far out into the calm bay there and spend the afternoon diving from the raft and scattering hundreds of tiny brightly coloured angel fish. Grand' Anse was different. It was isolated and uninhabited and sometimes she felt it had strayed to this island from somewhere else. You went down to it across a sandy plain where instead of palm trees there were casuarinas, their long pine needles combing the sky in the wind. Nowhere else on Mahé seemed to Julia to have as much wind as here, and the straight beach was pounded by breakers more power-ful than anywhere else on the island. They were strictly forbidden to cross the line of breakers to the waters that looked so calm beyond; there were dan-gerous currents there that would carry you away, far out to sea.

Grand' Anse was wonderful though for surfing, which was why they went there. They all had wooden boards, slightly curved at the front and almost as tall as themselves. You waited till a wave was about to break and launched yourself forward on the board. The wave caught you and sped you with it on its crest down and forward into the churning shallows, water bubbling and seething around you till your whole body was at the edge of the sea lying on the sand and

33

there was sand in your costume, in your eyes and in your hair.

Julia loved it. She loved the fast ride in and the struggle back out through the waves till the water in the shadow of the breaker was at her thighs and the breaker coming, curling, almost above her head. She loved the raging of the water, the roar of the wave as it broke. She raced her father, she raced Thomas and Marcel, she ran to rouse her resting mother and drag her in with them too.

Once she timed the curling of the wave badly and it tossed her round and round and sent her somersaulting and gasping for air. When she finally came up she saw her board being pulled out to sea and she tried to run after it but the water churned around her thighs and every time she took a step it pushed against her, stopping her from moving forward. Her father got to the board first and rescued it.

'I think we could all do with some food,' he said, 'come on, you lot.'

Two sandwiches later, Julia left the others eating and trailed down the warm sand till she reached the surf. Unlike at Beau Vallon, here they were forbidden to go into the sea alone. She sat down and gazed into the water, letting it run up her legs, as she bit into the hunk of dripping pineapple in her hand. Small shoals of tiny fish darted in and out of the surf. Gleefully she scooped up a handful of water and caught one in it. It was not much longer than her thumbnail. Trapped in her palm, it lay still for a moment and then, trembling with the effort, valiantly started to puff itself up to

34

frighten her, until it looked just like a small gaudy blue and yellow balloon. She laughed and dropped it back in the water where it instantly deflated and sped away.

She turned her head. Marcel and Thomas and her parents were still eating and talking. She got to her feet, called out, 'I'm going exploring,' waved and headed for the bluff at her side, sinking into the soft sand till she reached firmer ground. She smooched along the coast under the scattered casuarinas, enjoying the way the wind lifted her hair, scuffing her toes in the earth, picking cones off the ground and throwing them as far out to sea as she could.

She was just pulling back her arm to throw again when a strange sound came to her on the wind, a clanking noise. She lowered the cone and listened harder. Machinery was right out of place here. Curious, she began to walk towards the sound. She caught sight of a contraption of buckets on a chain belt juddering through the air and down.

She stared at it, thinking hard. Then she whirled and ran back the way she had come. Marcel and Thomas were at the water's edge digging up the sand where it bubbled to get at the 'tek-tek' below, small white shellfish that made delicious soup. Her parents seemed to be snoozing.

'Hey! Thomas-ss!' she whispered loudly.

Thomas looked up.

Urgently she signalled to them to come, one finger to her lips, the other hand beckoning. 'The treasure man! I think I've found the treasure man!' she said when they reached her. Her arms were twitching with excitement. 'Come and see. Down here.'

And they ran, bare feet padding on sandy soil. The tinny clanking of machinery grew louder. They stopped and squatted at the foot of a palm. Only a few yards away below them in a small bay, a pump was working. Each time it came up out of the sand, it released an arc of water into the trees with a whoosh. Down it went and up while the contraption of buckets on a chain belt juddered down into the pit, came up again, deposited the silt at the side, down again, on and round and down, clanging and banging. The pit was about as wide as Julia's bedroom floor. Rusting structures stood at the side like so much scrap iron. Rough, hand-painted notices warned people to keep away.

A scrawny man dressed only in a pair of oil-stained khaki shorts stood at the side of the pump making minor adjustments with a spanner, his back to them. They had seen him before but from the road, from inside a car and from a distance. They had never been this close. They had all heard the gossip about him, how he was rumoured to have given up a good job in France to come and treasure hunt. In the old days, before the French planters had arrived with their African slaves, the Seychelles had been uninhabited, visited only by pirates pausing in their raids on Arab shipping off the east coast of Africa. The man had found a map showing where treasure had been hidden, they said, but no one was sure since he talked to no one. He kept himself to himself.

The three children drew nearer. Turning, the man caught sight of them and frowned.

'Forbidden!' he shouted fiercely, waving his arms at them. 'Can't you read?' He jabbed at the nearest notice. '*Allez*! Go away! No children allowed!'

But Julia had caught sight of something on the ground between him and them. When he turned his back on them again, muttering loudly, she crept closer. The boys followed more cautiously.

She saw lacy petticoats stained with age, dark hair with a light covering of sand, arms and legs and faded eyes. She reached out a hand and touched. It was hard and cold.

The man span round and glared at them. 'Don't touch! That's not a toy! Can't you see that it's very old?' He lifted it and carefully blew sand off before placing it reverentially on an iron beam that ran above their heads. 'Kids nowadays,' he muttered. 'No respect.'

Julia, Marcel and Thomas stayed where they were. He stared at them perplexed. He had expected them to go.

'Is it a doll?' Julia asked. 'Where did you get it?'

He opened his mouth and shut it again. Then he began to talk in a loud and triumphant voice, a bit as if he was addressing a huge assembly. 'I found it this morning.' Emboldened by that he went on. 'They said I'd find nothing, but I did!'

The boasting passion in his strange shouting voice was scary. Julia wet her lips. The doll wasn't like any

37

she had seen before. They were toys; this one seemed real.

'How old is she?' she asked, looking up at it. The doll had a faded crimson dress on, fastened from top to bottom with tiny round pearl buttons.

'Eighteenth century,' he barked, softening for a moment, perhaps pleased to be sharing his find with someone, no matter how young. 'Almost two hundred years old. The pirates buried her facing east. It's a sign.' He stroked the doll, smiling, a funny twisted smile that only touched half his mouth, half his face; the other half stayed stiff and still. 'She's made of wax,' he confided. 'None of your modern plastic rubbish. Good wax.'

Julia started. She stared at him. She swallowed hard. The fun of the surfing had pushed thoughts of wax and candles and the greegree man out of her mind. 'Did – did the pirates make sacrifices too?' she squeaked. 'Was she a sacrifice?'

He glared. It was as if he were suddenly seeing them again. 'Bloody children! Always asking questions!' he exclaimed. 'What would you know about sacrifice!' He walked back to the pump. 'Go away!' he shouted over his shoulder. 'This is no place for kids. Go on, bugger off!' and then he came after them brandishing a spanner.

They turned tail and fled. When they emerged on to the hot sand at Grand' Anse, Julia and Thomas's mother was wading out to sea with a surfboard under her arm but their father was shooting to shore without one, his dark head leading, just visible through the frothing water. He came to a halt at the surf's edge, got up, shaking his head to clear his ears of water, and spotted them.

'We thought you'd gone off and left us!' he teased. 'Been anywhere interesting?'

Marcel, Thomas and Julia exchanged glances. Their meeting with the treasure man was something they wanted to keep to themselves. Thomas shook his head for all of them. Julia examined the pattern made by the edge of the surf at her feet, still worrying about the wax doll, wondering if there could be any link with greegree, any at all.

'Oh well,' their father said, looking amused, 'Come on then. I'll teach you to body surf.'

Their mother whooshed in at his side on her board and caught his last words. 'Will, are you sure?' she asked, getting to her feet. 'Aren't they a bit young?'

'Nonsense,' he said. 'And anyway, they're all strong swimmers. Aren't you?'

They nodded eagerly.

'Right then.' He demonstrated how they should launch themselves on the crest of the wave with a couple of crawl strokes to gain momentum. Once they felt the wave carry them, they were to tuck in their heads, press their arms to their sides and keep their legs together, as if they were themselves boards.

The first time Julia tried it she forgot to breathe properly and was tossed up half way, coughing and spluttering. By the third time Marcel and Thomas had got the knack. They had whooshed all the way in and she saw them capering joyously at the water's edge.

39

That put her on her mettle. She tried again and again. Then the right wave came, a wall of sea rising above her head, its tips beginning to whiten. Swiftly she turned to face the beach, and threw herself into the wave, her arms flailing in a crawl, then pushed against her sides, feet together, head in, and it was carrying her, gathering speed. Her hair was being lifted ahead of her. For a split second she hung above the churning water below, then the wave bore down with her in it, rushing forwards, and she was propelled through the roaring surf like a swift arrow skimming along its surface, water bubbling and churning all around her, on and on till she reached the warm, scratchy sand and felt the sun hot on her back.

CHAPTER 6

Julia was kneeling on sand, scrabbling desperately at
it, digging a hole, going deeper and deeper. The beach
beneath her was strangely cold and it chilled her legs
but still she dug, sure that there was something buried
down below. Her fingers touched lace. She pulled at
it. It was as fine and thin as cobwebs. She tugged at it
again and it came away in her fingers, more and more
of the stuff. Her fingers got caught in its holes, it
tangled itself around her hands. She fought with it and
won and it slithered away. She looked back in the hole
and plunged her hands back in deeper, digging more
carefully now. She touched something hard. She ·
brushed sand away from it. The old wax doll lay there,
staring up at her. She began gingerly to lift it out.
She had it in her arms. She looked up. Someone was
walking towards her. The treasure man. She heard
machinery now, whining and clanking, and there
were casuarina trees scattered on the horizon. The
treasure man drew closer. She put the doll back in the
hole and covered it quickly with sand before the
treasure man reached her, so that he wouldn't see it,
but he walked straight past as if she wasn't there,
shouting, though she couldn't hear a word he was
saying. Behind her the machinery grew louder and

louder and he kept shouting. She got to her feet and ran to escape but the soft sand stopped her, sucking at her ankles as she tried to move, heading for the sea, but there was no sea there. Instead there was a dark, menacing mass. The Hill. She wanted to go back the way she had come but she couldn't move. She twisted her head round and looked behind her. There was nothing there, no treasure man, only an empty beach. It was too empty. Desolate. And the whirring and clanking noise went on even though she could see no machinery. The noise swelled to a roar. She made a last huge effort to shift her feet and at last she broke free. She was out and running, straight ahead, right at The Hill. Just as she was almost there, it gave way and she was falling into water. Waves were all around her, churning and bubbling. She twisted and somersaulted and the roar of the waters was in her ears and the taste of salt was in her mouth. A wave came and lifted her higher and higher –

Julia woke with a jolt, heart hammering, mouth dry, eyes wide. It was dark! But her room shouldn't be dark, it was quite light, even at night. She shut her eyes in horror and swallowed hard.

Then she remembered that she now had curtains. That was the first bit of relief. She opened her eyes again, reached up for the corner of one and tugged it a little way open. Silver moonlight poured in from outside. She heard a snuffling sleeping noise and relaxed a little, recognizing the sounds of Simba their dog. She reached down and patted him where he lay sprawled on the cotton rug at the side of her bed. The dog

42

raised his head, licked her hand briefly and let his head drop again, sighing loudly. Simba wasn't supposed to sleep in the bedrooms but he often shuffled in when everyone was asleep and no one ever said anything.

It was all right, she told herself, her hand resting on the dog. Everything was all right. She was here in her bed. She was at home. She turned on to her side and began stroking Simba, reassured by the warm roughness of his coat. Her strokes grew more even and gradually the pounding of her heart subsided.

Her nightmare had been awful. From across the valley came the faint sound of voices calling, the bark of a distant dog, a clatter as of pans falling, the sounds of early morning. The images from the dream were beginning to fade. Already she could no longer see the lopsided smile on the treasure man's face.

She took a deep breath and threw back her sheet. She stepped over Simba and went to her parents' room, in through the open doorway, wanting a cuddle. There was no movement in the bed, just one motionless mound with two heads. She took a step forward. As she did so, a streak of light appeared in the sky outside their window.

Dawn came suddenly in the tropics. She hesitated, then turned and ran back across the hall to her bedroom. She grabbed her tin of treasures from the floor, climbed through the open window and, deliberately not looking at The Hill, jumped to the ground and ran round the corner of the bungalow to her brother's window-sill. It was the best place for watching dawn.

43

She hoisted herself up and – avoiding the mud mason-fly nest in the corner so as not to be stung – put one foot into the wall where the uneven granite left a foothold. She peeped in to check that Thomas was still sleeping. For this, she wanted to be alone.

St Anne island opposite at the outer edge of the harbour was already showing black against yellow. Julia clasped her knees and watched the sun come up. The island darkened more blackly and then sprang to life as the gold turned to white and then blue, a vast vivid blue, as the sun came right up and over the top of St Anne to flood the world with its glorious primitive light, chasing away the darkness. She felt as if she was watching a magical play put on specially for her, the only spectator in a vast auditorium. 'Let there be light,' she said to herself, and beamed, her fears pushed away too.

There was still about an hour until breakfast. She turned to the round toffee tin and emptied its contents beside her. There was a lizard that months before had dropped dead from the ceiling right on to her tummy as she lay in bed watching it. Now it was old and dried. She put it on the back of her hand and closed her eyes. It was true, she couldn't feel it. If she didn't know she had just put it on the back of her hand, she would open her eyes and there'd be nothing. She put it down on the window-sill and unwrapped tissue paper. Inside, still undamaged, was the skeleton of the cinnamon leaf that she'd taken from the garden path. Then there were two teeth, one hers, one Thomas's. She frowned; she didn't think his tooth really belonged here. She twisted round to face the bedroom, aimed carefully and threw it at him. It didn't matter now if Thomas woke up. It landed near his arm but he didn't stir.

She turned back to her final treasure: her lucky bean. A round, red compeche seed, hollowed out and filled with tiny animals. She pulled out the delicate ivory plug and gently shook the contents on to the lid of her toffee tin. She licked her finger and pressed it on to each animal in turn in order to lift it up and examine it more closely: a giraffe, its slender neck stretching; a lion poised to spring; two antelope caught in mid-flight; an elephant, its trunk waving; another giraffe, its legs even longer than the first; a puzzled-looking buffalo; a lumbering rhinoceros with horn pointing skywards; all were exquisitely carved from ivory, and each one only half the size of her little finger nail. As she finished gazing at each, she returned it to its dark home, sliding it in off her finger, careful not to drop it. When they were all safely back inside, she plugged the bean shut once more.

She sat a little longer, clasping her toes in her hands, trying to decide what to do next. She turned her head and peered in at Thomas. He was still sleeping, the tooth on the pillow near his cheek. She caught her breath. It was silly of her to have chucked it away, even if it was his. It had been in her collection for at least a year; why reject it today? She swivelled round on the sill and jumped down lightly on to the floor. She tiptoed over to his bed and retrieved it, pleased that he hadn't woken.

She scrambled back up to the sill, paused to put the tooth next to her own, and jumped down to the grass, leaving her treasures where they were. She ran to the other end of the bungalow, stopping only to poke her finger through the wire netting of the chicken run and cluck at the hens, past Thérèse's room, its door still closed, and into the kitchen. She was hungry, she realized.

Skirting the corner near the old range where the cockroaches lurked, she took a mango and knife, and went back to Thomas's window-sill. She watched the black-and-white funnelled ship anchored out in the bay. It had arrived yesterday from Mombasa for a three-day stay before continuing on its way from Africa to India. Already smaller boats were bustling out to it for the day's trade.

She held the mango in her left hand, then picked up the knife and sliced through the taut mango skin. The juice oozed out at once. She pulled her nightdress tightly across her knees to form a bowl in her lap and catch the juice. Now she criss-crossed each half, put down the knife and turned the skin inside out, making the golden lumps of flesh stand out. Slowly she sucked each delicious square, oblivious to the juice running down her arms and now through her nightdress to trickle down her thighs.

She closed her eyes, relishing the sweet, musty taste. She licked her fingers clean. She rubbed them on her nightgown to make sure and then she put everything back in her treasure tin – and closed the lid.

*

46

'All right, next question. What's the capital of Kenya?'

'Nairobi,' Julia and Thomas called together.

Julia's father looked across at their mother who was keeping score. 'I think Thomas got in first.'

Julia pushed her empty plate out of the way and rested her elbows on the table so that she could concentrate better. They'd been to church, they'd been swimming at Beau Vallon and now they'd come home for a specially big tea. After tea she and Thomas had asked for a game. A quiz then, her father had suggested, and they'd agreed. Mainly on geography, he'd said.

'Where do our cotton sheets come from?'

'England. No, India,' said Thomas.

'Egypt,' shouted Julia.

'Ah. Well it could be either –' he said looking at their mother.

'India,' she said. 'But I think you can both have a point.'

'Name the most southerly bay on Mahé,' their father said. There was a long pause.

Thomas said cautiously, 'Lazare?'

'Julia? Which do you think?' Their father looked at her. 'As far south as you can go.'

'Anse Intendance?' she asked.

'No, it's Police Bay. Now how about the five highest mountains.'

'Trois Frères,' they chorused.

'That's three. The other two?'

'Morne Seychellois,' said Thomas first.

47

'Yes. And the fifth?'

There was a long silence.

'Come on, what's the name of the mountain behind us? Well, hill really.'

Thomas span his knife on the table top and didn't look up. Julia stared at the knife.

'What is the matter with you two? You do know it,' their father said encouragingly.

Julia wondered if that could be true. She supposed so, but all she could think of was The Hill and she wasn't going to say that.

Her father sighed. 'Morne Souci,' he said, 'It's Morne Souci. Perhaps that's enough for today.' He stretched his arms and yawned. 'What's the score, Elizabeth?'

'Morne Souci,' Julia thought. So it did have a real name.

'Thomas has seventeen, and Julia – fourteen,' said their mother, totting up the figures.

Julia automatically pulled a face at Thomas for winning but he didn't pull one back. He was looking bothered.

Their parents got up from the table.

'I'm going to look at the tadpoles,' Julia said meaningfully at Thomas.

Thomas nodded and came out with her, across the back lawn, past Julia's guava tree, and down on to the terraces where the tomatoes grew, tied to stakes. There was water between the terraces and tadpoles in one of the shallow ditches there. They squatted down to watch them. Julia put her hand in the water and felt them tickle her fingers as they swam across.

'Thomas –' she started.

'No.'

'What do you mean, no? You don't know what I was going to say.'

'Yes, I do. You were going to say something about The Hill and the other night. I don't want to talk about it, I really don't.'

'No I wasn't.' She glared at him. 'I've got an idea.'

He looked warily at her.

'Let's go down to the bottom of the terraces and shout, "Morne Souci" at The Hill.'

Thomas stood up. 'No.'

'Why not?' She stood up too and faced him. But he was walking back up the terraces.

'Thomas!' she called.

'I'm going to read,' he shouted back, waving at her.

You're still scared, she thought to herself. Then she would have to do it on her own.

She went down to the bottom of the garden and gazed up at The Hill. 'Morne Souci,' she thought again to herself, giving herself courage. She cupped her hands round her mouth.

'Morne Souci!' she shouted. 'Morne Souci!' she taunted it. 'Morne Souci!' and a bird near her stopped singing.

'Morne Souci!' she called again defiantly.

It didn't help. She drooped a bit. She had thought that calling The Hill by its official name would make it less scary. It didn't. It was still as dark as it had been in her dream.

'Morne Souci,' she said in her normal speaking

49

voice. It was still The Hill to her, The Hill where they said the greegree man might catch you.

She span round and ran up the garden to find Thérèse, who was unlatching the door to the chicken run outside the kitchen. She slipped inside with her, panting. She collected eggs where the hens had laid them in the straw while Thérèse scattered grain on the earth.

Julia carried the eggs into the kitchen. When she came out again on to the back verandah, Thérèse was taking out the coconut husk polishers.

Julia perched on the table beside her as she unscrewed the large flat tin of red Mansion polish. She began to talk, to babble, about anything at all. 'We saw the treasure man yesterday,' she told her, 'me and Marcel and Thomas.'

'Uh-huh,' said Thérèse, rubbing the exposed bristle of the husk into the polish.

'He's not far from Grand' Anse,' she went on. 'I'd thought he was *miles* away but he's not.'

Now Thérèse was doing the same to the second husk. She didn't seem especially interested in the subject of the treasure man.

'He's found a doll,' Julia persisted.

Thérèse paused. 'Really? What sort of doll?'

'Very ancient. He told us it's nearly two hundred years old. It was made of wax.' She watched carefully to see if Thérèse would react to the word wax.

Thérèse only looked surprised. 'He actually talked to you?'

Julia nodded. 'He chased us away afterwards.'

Thérèse put the lid back on the tin and screwed it shut. 'Well,' she said. 'You were honoured.'

'Thérèse.'

'Mmm?' She didn't look up.

'Have you ever seen the greegree man?' Julia held her breath, not sure if Thérèse would answer.

Thérèse looked searchingly at her. 'No,' she said abruptly.

'Has anyone?'

Thérèse picked up the two husk polishers. 'I don't know,' she said, 'and I'm not asking. And the subject is closed.'

'What do you think he looks like?' Julia persevered quickly.

Thérèse frowned. 'How can I know if I haven't seen him? No more now, Julia. I told you. Stop thinking about it.'

How could she? Julia thought. Thérèse being so secretive scared her.

'Look,' Thérèse went on, 'I have to get on and polish the dining-room floor. You can help if you like.'

Julia followed her into the dining room and watched as Thérèse started off, pushing the coconut-husk polisher back and forth with her foot.

Julia joined in beside her with her own husk, swivelling on her left foot while pushing out on the husk with her right. She concentrated hard, swivel push, swivel push, clumsy at first then more graceful, swivel sweep, hands behind her back like Thérèse, dancing over the already shining red floor, and with each stroke came an image, not jumbled up as in her dream

51

but separate now, the treasure man, the wax doll, the sea, wax, Thérèse not wanting to talk, candles, her father saying Morne Souci not knowing, Thérèse, The Hill, greegree.

CHAPTER 7

The minute she heard the tinkle of the rickshaw bell in the drive Julia slipped from her seat at the breakfast table, kissed her mother and father goodbye, picked up her sandals and school straw hat and left quickly before Thomas could tease her. Since her attack of pneumonia her parents had ordered a rickshaw to come and fetch her every day for school and take her home again while they were at work, even though she was better now. Thomas who walked, as she had used to do, made her feel like a baby for still being taken to school.

'*Bonjour*, Pierre. Good morning.' She sat on the cracked leather seat under the canopy. Its fringe of blue and green beads shook gently in her face.

''*Jour*, Julia.' Pierre picked up the shafts of the rickshaw and set off down the drive. Julia watched the gold earring in his right ear flash and twinkle as the sun bounced off it. Pierre must be old, she thought. His crinkly hair was grey but once when she'd asked him how old he was he'd cackled and said he wasn't a grandfather yet even though the oldest of his nine children was sixteen.

On they went down the hill, passing the woman with elephantiasis who was struggling up it as she did every morning at this time, her monstrously swollen left leg dragging behind her. Julia twisted round in her seat and watched her, wondering how anyone could manage to walk with a leg four times its normal size. They went past the Botanical Gardens where you could ride on giant land tortoises as high as your waist and more than a hundred years old. The road changed to tarmac.

There was a roar, a rush of wind at Julia's elbow, and a screech of tyres. A motorbike, black and gleaming, missed them by inches. It slewed to an undignified halt on its side ahead of them. The rider got up slowly, unhurt but clearly shaken.

Pierre dropped the shafts in the road, nearly throwing Julia off the seat, and leaped over to the young man. '*Cochon!*' he shouted. 'Tit of a pig! You nearly killed us! Where's your licence? Let's see your licence!'

'Keep your bald patch on, Grandad,' the young man sneered, getting up and rubbing his leg. He took out a handkerchief and tenderly began wiping down the side of the motorbike where it had scraped on the road. 'At least I have a licence. You don't even know the meaning of the word with that rickshaw.'

Cyclists, pedestrians, even the beggars from the steps of the Indian shop opposite were beginning to press round, eager to see what might happen next. Julia left the rickshaw and joined the edge of the crowd.

Pierre was dancing with rage, his elbows sticking out at right angles. 'I was at the side of the road, perfectly safe till you came along,' he yelled.

54

Julia nodded in confirmation though no one was looking at her.

'You should stick with things your own size,' Pierre went on. 'They should never have let you off your mother's lap!'

Julia listened with interest. She'd never known Pierre angry before. The young man began furiously wiping the mudguard.

'What the devil do you think you were doing, driving that close?' demanded Pierre, pushing his face against the motorcyclist's.

'He came out from the side street,' one beggar said helpfully, a gleeful smile on his pocked face. 'Wasn't looking. Going far too fast.'

'Count yourself lucky I didn't run you over, Grandad,' taunted the young man, polishing his handlebars now.

'*Ferme ta gueule, conkéla!*' Pierre screamed at him.

'Who do you think you're calling a cockroach?' the man shouted back, standing straight now and bristling. 'You, the brother of a rat, nephew of a whore!'

Pierre spat. A large gobbet landed, trembling and glistening, in the road between their feet. He raised his hand. 'Son of a –'

A whistle blew shrilly. The crowd muttered and stirred as a policeman strode through, all khaki and shining leather. He pulled the men apart.

'Pierre Lafont? This isn't like you, old man, brawling in the street.' He took him by the arm. 'Get back to your rickshaw.'

Pierre didn't budge.

'You heard me. Go on.' He gave him a push.

Julia nipped away ahead of Pierre and sat in the rickshaw as he approached reluctantly, hurling curses over his shoulder. He didn't look at her. He picked up the rickshaw and began to move. They drew level with the policeman and the young man.

'*Al faire foute ou maman!*' Pierre cursed loudly, and finally, over his shoulder as they passed. He broke into a vigorous trot.

'Oh!' Julia put her hand to her mouth and giggled. That was the worst thing you could say to anyone. And Pierre had said it! She watched his feet pound the road, saw how he held his head high and decided to keep perfectly quiet.

The road got busier. Some cars overtook them now. Most people were on bicycles though, or walking. They went past the market. Pierre's speed began to slacken and his shoulder bones to look less rigid under his shirt. He even called out a greeting to another rickshaw driver. Julia relaxed.

They approached the cathedral. Julia put on one sandal and then the other and pressed her hat on her head. She glanced up at the clock at the same time as Pierre. A quarter past eight. Fifteen minutes early, despite the motorcyclist. The Devil's clock said a quarter to twelve. Pierre set down the shafts of the rickshaw on the far side of the cathedral where the tarmac gave way to dirt road again.

'I've seen him at my brother's,' Pierre said, turning to her.

'Who?' asked Julia.

'Jules Laroche. That nutter. He's no good. He's been to Mauritius. When he came back he was no good.'

'Oh.' She slid across to the corner of the seat.

'First accident I've ever had.' He looked at her indignantly. 'Never had one in my life before. Not in thirty-two years of being a rickshaw driver. Not till today,' he went on, muttering half to himself now. 'Don't know why it should have happened today.'

Julia's heart sank. Oh no, she thought. Maybe it had something to do with her.

'Nothing wrong with me and my rickshaw,' he went on. 'Just a bit of bad luck me being on the road then. Bad luck.'

Julia sat still, not saying a word. What if she was right, what if she had brought him bad luck?

He perched on the seat beside her, rolled a thin cigarette in two swift movements and lit it. 'I'll tell my brother he can't have Jules round again,' Pierre said suddenly.

Julia nodded, relieved that Pierre had found a solution. She watched him smoking his cigarette. When he got halfway down it, he began to talk. His wife had won money at the church tombola, he told her. She settled into her seat to listen. She always enjoyed his vivid monologues of what he had been up to at the weekend. She thought this was often the best part of the ride. But this time she couldn't concentrate. She watched his lips move but only heard half of what he said. He had caught his second daughter's boyfriend in the room alone with her, he was telling Julia, and had chased him out (here he looked fiercely at her). He and his brother had got drunk on palm wine during a –

Now Julia was alert. She held her breath. He paused. 'During a what, Pierre?' she asked finally, watching him watch the smoke twirl away from his cigarette.

'Nothing you should know about, little girl,' he answered abruptly.

She wrinkled her nose at him.

'Pierre,' she said, needing to ask. 'Pierre – are you and your brother friends? I mean, will he talk to you?'

'Will Edouard talk to me? Yes, of course,' he answered, surprised. 'He was over yesterday when Brigitte was cutting firewood and he said that it was like –'

This time she interrupted him. 'That's not really what I mean. What I mean is – what do you do if you want to talk and he doesn't?'

Pierre looked thoughtful. 'That depends,' he said. 'Is this about me? Or is it about you and Thomas?'

She had been right to think he would understand.

'What is it you want to talk to him about?'

'I – I'm not allowed to say.' She badly wanted to.

'Something secret?' he asked.

She nodded.

'Best left alone,' he advised her. 'If he doesn't want to, then best forget it.'

Julia sighed.

At that moment two of her school mates from St Joseph's came past, their tunics, unlike hers, elegantly faded to a cloudy blue, the pleats less sharply pressed, no hats on their heads. She saw them nudge each other and laugh. Quickly she took her hat off and twirled it in her fingers. She hated being seen in the rickshaw.

'Pierre,' she said. 'I think –'

He nodded. He picked up the rickshaw again and took her the last few hundred yards to school while behind him on the seat Julia debated to herself whether Pierre's stories were worth the embarrassment of turning up this way each morning. She suspected that her parents had simply forgotten that she used to be allowed to walk.

'Pierre,' she said when he stopped. 'I can come and talk to you at the market, can't I?'

'Yes.' He looked surprised. 'I don't see why not,' he said.

'I mean, I don't have to be your passenger for you to talk to me, do I?' she went on, not wanting to hurt his feelings.

'No,' he agreed.

'Then please don't come for me this afternoon,' she said as she got out of the rickshaw. 'Please. I'm better now. I can walk home.' Besides, she thought, if their accident had somehow been because of her, he'd be better off without her.

He hesitated.

'Really. I'll tell Maman and Papa.' She watched him, worried that he wouldn't agree, but to her relief he did.

'You be sure to come and say hello,' he said sternly. Then he held out his hand, smiling, and they shook on

59

it. He turned back in the direction of the market to wait for customers.

Julia joined the girls filing in to her classroom, a simple wooden hut like the others dotted around the dusty plain, raised up on stones in an effort to prevent the white ants from eating it as they had eaten the fur off Thomas's teddy bear. She went to her desk near the middle and stood behind her chair. A breeze brushed her cheek on its way from the open doorway to the open window on the other side.

'Psst!' hissed Antoinette, and Julia turned round and smiled as Antoinette winked. She caught Cécile's eye too and waved a finger at her before turning back quickly.

The nun up on the platform was waiting till they were all in and standing in silence. She made the sign of the cross and started to lead them in prayer.

Julia crossed herself like the others, hand to forehead, left, right, middle and hands folded. '*Au nom du Père et du Fils et du Saint Esprit*. In the name of the Father and of the Son and of the Holy Ghost,' she recited in French, the language they used for prayers at school though the lessons were in English. She had got used to making the sign of the cross at school and praying between each lesson.

Twenty wooden chairs were drawn back on the wooden floor; twenty girls sat down for geography. Gondwanaland, Sister John told them, drawing a map of a vast lost continent on the blackboard, had once stretched all the way from Africa across to India and Australia. The Seychelles islands were almost all that was left of that ancient land, she said; where they were now had once been the mountain tops of Gondwana-land, as high then as Mount Everest is now.

Cécile, at Julia's side, giggled and raised her eyes to the palm-fronded roof. 'Land doesn't just disappear!' she whispered in Creole to Julia.

But Julia was listening carefully to Sister John. She thought she believed Sister John with her lined face and her sensible, brown laced-up shoes that gleamed with polish where they peeped out from under the hem of her white habit. She suspected that the hair under Sister John's white veil would be grey, if there was any there at all. Yes, she believed her. First there had been the pirates. Then Frenchmen had arrived with their families. They had brought slaves over with them from Africa in the eighteenth century to cultivate coconuts and sugar cane, vanilla for flavouring and sweet-smelling patchouli for perfume. The slaves and landowners had ended up blending their language and their children; the barriers between the races became blurred and the children more mixed. Cécile had an Indian grandparent whose father had come to work in the plantations when many freed slaves refused to, and Antoinette, whose eyes slanted when she laughed, had a mother who was Chinese; she ran one of the two grocery shops in Port Victoria, near the market. Finally the colony had passed into the hands of the British, which was why Julia was here.

All this and more Julia had been told, and now, even further back, far older than habitation, there was Gondwanaland. She frowned, trying to imagine land where now there was sea; fields and cultivated terraces where today the waves came crashing in.

If Sister John knew about how The Hill was formed, she thought suddenly, she might be able to tell her more about candles and greegree. When it was break and they were told to go out and play, she approached the teacher's desk and hovered.

'Yes, Julia?' The serious face looked at her. 'What is it? Is there something you didn't understand?'

Julia shook her head. 'No. I mean yes,' she corrected herself. 'When we were Gondwanaland, when this was all mountains, was there gree—'

She stopped. The nun's eyes had widened, she had put down the pen in her hand and stiffened.

Julia wished she hadn't spoken. The last time she had offended Sister John, she'd had to spend all break kneeling on the ground outside, not allowed to speak to anyone.

'I hope I didn't hear what I think I was beginning to hear, mmm?'

'No, Sister.' Julia's eyes slipped away from the nun's.

'I don't ever want to hear that word you might have been about to mention again. Ever.'

Julia headed for the open doorway, trying her hardest to walk at a normal pace and not run. She knew that if she turned round she would see Sister John staring at her. She could feel her eyes now on the back of her neck.

Two steps down and she was on the ground, the sun on her head. She needed to find out more about greegree but no one would tell. All the class huts were empty now for break and the school yard was littered with huddles of squatting girls, absorbed in their games of 'conoche', stone clinking on stone. Antoinette and Cécile were in a small group at the far side in the shade of a mango tree. Marie was with them. Everything was quite as usual. And yet, thought Julia, it was as if they were on one side of a glass wall and she was on the other. If only she had never gone up The Hill. There was a strangeness about some things now that she didn't remember being there before, and she wished it would go away.

She turned back towards the classroom, nervous but determined. She had to try Sister John again. She had to find out more. She walked up to the desk.

'Sister –' she began, and then the words tumbled out, 'Is greegree as old as Christianity?'

Sister John pushed back her chair and got up. 'Is it older?' Julia insisted, desperately.

'The subject is closed, Julia,' the nun said, putting her papers together, her lips set tightly. 'There is no such thing.'

But Julia knew she was wrong or, worse, lying. 'That's not true! There is!' She cried, standing her ground.

'Julia! Don't be so cheeky! I do not know what is wrong with you. Go out and play with the others this instant before I put you in detention. Go on – out!'

Julia stood outside again, tears pricking the backs of her eyelids. She was right; she knew she was. Of course greegree existed. And she wished the strange-ness would go away. Between Julia and the others was the long hut without windows where the lavatories were, eight dark, smelly pits with wooden seats over them, divided by partitions. Julia turned to go there now. She thought it might bring herself back to earth. She paused in the open doorway at one end, wrinkling up her nose at the smell. The first two cubicles were occupied; the third was empty. She was good at hold-ing her breath from swimming underwater; her record was holding it for a minute. She had learned to time her visits to the lavatory accordingly. Now she took a deep breath, opened the door, lifted the round lid off the pit and perched, ignoring spiders and ants, put back the lid, opened the door again and was almost out at the far end of the long hut before she released the last bit of air and breathed in again. A tap stood outside the door, permanently half open, trickling a stream of water across the dusty ground. Julia rinsed her hands, dried them on her tunic and went over to the others, ignoring the chicken that jumped out of her path, cackling in alarm. Miraculously, the strange feeling had quite left her.

She joined her friends playing 'conoche' and took her turn after Marie, catching the stones on the hol-lowed back of her hand, throwing them up in the air, catching them, tossing them back, once, twice, six times without letting a single one fall.

'Can you come and stay this week?' Marie asked Julia. Her eyes were exactly the colour of the sky behind her, Julia thought. Distracted, she dropped a

64

stone. She grimaced and pushed them all over to Antoinette.

'I think so. I'll ask,' she replied. 'Do you know what Thomas and I did the other night?' she began, for an instant not thinking. The strange feeling rushed back. She had promised Thérèse not to tell and now the words stuck in her throat. She was relieved to see Sister Agatha come out just at that moment ringing the big bell. They picked up the stones and she was able to take refuge in the silence as they trooped back inside to the classroom. '*Marie, mère de Dieu, priez pour nous.* Holy Mary, Mother of God, pray for us,' crossing themselves, sitting down again. Then chanting the endings of a French verb in unison: '*J'aimais, tu aimais, il aimait, nous aimions, vous aimiez, ils aimaient.*' The voices rose and fell as if in song, as Sister Dominic prompted from the blackboard. The verb finished, the voices stopped. But the words didn't; 'I love, you love, he loves,' went on round and round in Julia's head, like a spell, stopping her from concentrating on the dictation they were being given.

Sister Dominic broke off at the end of a sentence and Julia looked up in relief. Josephine's mother stood in the doorway, a baby in her arms. The nun nodded to her and she came into the classroom and gave Josephine the child. Josephine unbuttoned her blouse and put the baby to her breast, smiling shyly. Sister Dominic rubbed the verbs from the blackboard and began to draw a diagram explaining exactly how milk was produced after birth in the human mother and in all mammals. Josephine was a good four years older

65

than most girls in the class. Throughout her pregnancy, hygiene lessons had turned into sessions about how the baby was growing in her tummy, the nun as excited by it all as they had been. Josephine had not told any of them who the father was.

CHAPTER 8

Julia and Cécile walked down Long Pier with nothing on either side but the sea gently lapping, nothing ahead but the long raised concrete jetty the width of one car leading into the deeper sea, glaring harshly in the afternoon sun. Cécile almost always came to meet her father after school. He worked in the customs shed right at the end of the pier. Julia sometimes came with her to see the turtles.

She undid the buttons of her belt and trailed it in her hand; it was cooler so with her school tunic falling loose.

On they walked, the sun bouncing off the pier. Twice Julia had had a nightmare in which she was walking down a pier which slowly sank to the level of the water. Tiny waves rippled over it and soon covered it. When she looked down at her feet she could still see the concrete through the clear water, but not when she gazed ahead at the vast expanse of empty sea. She knew she could not turn back; she had to keep walking along the buried road, trusting, hoping with each step that she would touch ground.

'Watch out!' She jumped out of her reverie. She was in the middle of the pier and in the way of two fishermen who were bearing down on them at a trot. Cécile had already moved neatly to the side and was laughing at her. She joined her quickly just as the men padded past, hips swivelling, knees bent, curved knives in their free hands looking like an extension of their arms. Their other hands supported a pole that was slung across their shoulders and from it hung a row of red and silver bourgeois fish, tied to it with string threaded through their gills.

When they had gone past, the girls drifted back into the middle of the road. The high masts of the schooners moored at the end of the pier were growing taller and the low customs shed larger. On the left at the end, opposite it and jutting out into the sea, was what looked like a large swimming pool, a swimming pool left to rot, for the water was a dirty brown, the shallow concrete steps at one end thick with slime. It stank with the stench of rotting fish and stale urine. In the pool, turtles swam up and down, round and round, trapped in their dirty prison. Only a wall separated them from the clear turquoise sea where they had been caught, which stretched and glittered on the other side. If she were in charge of their watery prison, Julia thought, their water would be clean every day.

Julia and Cécile perched three steps up from the level of the water and watched for a turtle to surface. This was not a place where adults came; perhaps they could not bear the stench. Julia didn't mind it all that much; she thought the lavatories at school were worse.

Turtles could swim for a long time before needing to come up for air. Sometimes the pool was full and you didn't have to wait long to see one; at other times there were only two or three and there would be long gaps between each sighting. The water was so murky that no matter how carefully you looked you could not make out the turtles until they were about to emerge. At last their patience was rewarded. Julia nudged Cécile and pointed: a blurred shape was moving below them. It came closer to the surface, showing the top of its stumpy head. Two pairs of powerful flippers thrashed the water. Out came the leathery head to breathe. Two eyes peered sorrowfully at them. The turtle seemed to consider, then its mouth slowly opened in a loud gasp and back it sank in the water to continue its futile swimming, round and round.

'My Dad says their meat tastes really good,' Cécile said dolefully.

Julia was surprised. 'I thought they were caught for their shells.'

'So did I,' Cécile said, 'till yesterday. That's another sort of turtle. Dad says these ones are caught for their meat and fat.'

'Oh,' said Julia, reminded by the mention of fat and distracted for a moment from the poor turtles. 'Cécile, what does your father do with the wax from his honeycombs?'

'He eats it,' Cécile said. 'You know that. You had some.'

'Yes. But doesn't he use any to make candles with?'

'Whatever for? Look, there –'

There was a rush of water not far away from them. They watched a turtle gulp in air, moaning loudly, and sink back into the water.

'Well, will you ask him?' Julia asked when the water had subsided again.

'All right.' Cécile rubbed her nose absentmindedly.

'As soon as he comes out? And tell me tomorrow. OK?' She was like a terrier with a rat, not letting go.

Cécile nodded, scanning the water.

Julia wandered off down the edge of the pool, back to where it joined the pier. She rounded the corner of a shed and stopped. A cart was standing there. On it was a layer of turtles turned on their backs and tied to the cart with rope. On top of this was another layer of turtles on their backs, and more rope. And a third layer. Julia had seen the cart here before, standing like that close to the pool waiting to be pulled away, but never with so many layers of turtles. There they lay in the merciless heat. Occasionally a flipper made a weak swimming movement. Tears dripped from their eyes. Julia's eyes began watering too in sympathy. She swallowed hard.

She turned away and hunted around until she found a small pile of discarded coconut shells. Then she fetched Cécile.

'Come and help me water the turtles,' she pleaded, but Cécile needed no persuasion. They lay on their tummies and leaned over the edge of the pier trying to reach the sea for fresh water, but even Julia's arms were just too short. So they went to the turtle pool and carefully carried shellful after shellful of the dirty water to the cart and poured it over the turtles in an attempt to moisten them.

'Do you think it's helping?' Julia asked anxiously, examining one of the suffering turtles closely, noticing the dullness of its wrinkled skin.

'A bit,' Cécile said hopefully.

They went back to the pool for another lot of water. Julia caught Cécile glancing up at the mountains.

'Have you ever gone up that hill?' she asked, the words coming out in a rush.

Cécile stopped and stared at Julia. 'Which hill?'

'That one. Up there. You know.' Julia pointed.

'Of course not!' Cécile retorted. 'No one goes up there.'

She dipped the shell into the pool.

Julia knelt beside her and dipped too.

'What happens if they do?' Julia asked her. Just to check.

They began carrying the shells back to the turtles.

'Awful things,' Cécile said at last. 'Terrible things. I'd die rather than go up there.'

Some water from Julia's coconut shell splashed to the ground. She felt sick. The smell coming off the turtles wasn't helping.

A man had come out of the shed as they approached. He moved to stand between them and the turtles, and stared pointedly at them. They faltered then stopped. They stood uncertainly then headed back to the pool. Cécile sat down again.

'I think I'll go home,' Julia said, hovering, wanting

to be away from the smell. 'You will remember to ask your father, won't you?'

'Ask him what?' Cécile answered, squinting up at her, shielding her eyes from the sun.

'About the wax.' Julia said impatiently. 'And candles.'

'Oh that,' Cécile said. 'Yes, all right.'

Julia dawdled up the hill on the way home. She was feeling better now. The sun, hot and familiar on her back, soothed her. There were plenty of cashew trees on the way and she stopped to pick out the nuts from the red fruit that lay bruised at the roadside. She had missed this all those weeks when she'd been in the rickshaw. She made a pouch of her tunic and put the nuts in it. A woman came past, walking steadily, a laundry basket balanced on her head. Julia watched her go then stepped lightly out into the road in her wake. Holding her tunic with its cargo of nuts carefully with her left hand, she tried to copy the woman's graceful swaying motion but her clothes were all wrong, and so were her legs. If only she was older, she thought, and larger in the right places, and wearing a long, draping skirt with flounces round the bottom, she might be better at it.

A narrow overgrown path sneaked off through the trees to the right. Julia paused, then decided to take it. Here banana trees grew close together, their clutches of small, yellow bananas only a little higher than her head. It was the spiders that made the walk adventurous, black hairy ones which spun their webs right

72

across the path. The trick was to spot them in time so that you didn't touch the tacky mess and furry legs. Not scared now that it was daylight, Julia picked a twig from the ground and tickled one particularly large spider, its body about the size of her fist. It moved in a stately sort of way to the far corner of its web, as if it had been about to move all the time.

Still holding on to her tunic pouch with her left hand, Julia stood to attention and addressed the spider.

'I have important news, my liege.' She had two lines to say in *Joan of Arc*, the school play. Saint Joan of Arc, the nuns called her, stressing the 'saint'. She and Marie and Cécile were heralds. She cleared her throat and tried the line again in a deeper voice. 'I have important news. My liege.'

The spider stared at her unwinkingly. She saluted it, beginning to feel a bit foolish, wishing it would react. It didn't; it went on staring at her, as if it knew something.

She shivered. She ducked under the web and carried on until she came out at the wider path which was the usual short cut through to home. She plucked a leaf from one of the cinnamon bushes on either side and twirled it between thumb and forefinger of her right hand, thinking. What she had done was surely not so terrible, she thought, not really. She and Thomas had climbed The Hill and they shouldn't have done, but the greegree man hadn't in fact caught them. Here she was in their own grounds. So why was she so anxious?

She crushed the leaf and bent her head to breathe in

its bittersweet smell. That comforted her a little. The leaf skeleton in her treasure tin had come from this path; she had picked it from one of the bushes where it had already dried, perfect in its tracery.

Emerging at last into the garden, she flung herself down on the grass, releasing the nuts from her tunic and sending them tumbling to the ground in a heap. A couple knocked a 'sensitive plant' and she watched it curl its tiny leaves up tightly, shocked at being disturbed.

'The Dauphin is marching this way,' she muttered, trying out her second line, making herself think about the play again. Though really, she thought, it was silly to practise without Cécile or Marie there; they were going to have to say the lines in unison. The grass itched, a pleasant sort of itch. She picked a blade and examined its edge, just like a saw with its teeth. If the teeth made her itch, what would they do to the fragile leg of an insect? she wondered.

A hand snaked down and took some cashew nuts from her pile.

'Oh!' She sat up, surprised.

'I was looking for you,' Thomas said. 'I want to show you something. Are you coming?'

'What is it?' she asked, standing up.

He beckoned mysteriously and set off along the terrace below her guava tree and the staked tomatoes, so that they couldn't be seen from the kitchen. When he judged they'd reached the end of the house, he led her through some bushes and pushed them aside at a small hut which was the servants' lavatory.

Thomas pointed. 'There,' he said, flicking hair from his eyes.

Julia stood on tiptoe to see what he was pointing at: a large pinky red flower with flat wide petals and purple stamens in the middle. It looked frail and yet strangely tough too. Behind it loomed The Hill. She tried to ignore it and concentrate on the flower.

'It's been there for days,' he said.

She was puzzled. 'So?' It wasn't like Thomas to make a fuss about a flower.

'So,' he was impatient with her now. 'Have you never noticed how quickly flowers die? Most of them are gone within a day. This one isn't dying. I've been watching it.'

She tried to reach it, to see what it felt like.

'Don't touch it!'

'I can't anyway!' she retorted. He was already returning through the bushes, clearly expecting her to follow. Instead she went round and tried reaching the flower from another angle but could get no closer. She examined it as best she could, puzzled, and then trailed down the path towards the kitchen steps. Thérèse was there, head down, whittling at a palm leaf, making toothpicks. Julia sat down beside her and took the knife and long leaf from her.

'Come to help, *chérie*?'

She nodded. Thérèse got up to go.

'No, stay.' Julia tugged at her skirt. 'Why doesn't that flower down by your lavatory die?'

'What flower?' Thérèse asked.

'The strange one. High up. Big.'

75

'What were you doing down there? It's private.'

'Sorry,' she muttered automatically, whittling away, not really sorry at all.

'You should go and get changed,' Thérèse said. 'What have you been doing? Your tunic's filthy.'

Julia looked down at the stains on the front and pulled a face. 'It's the turtles' water,' she said. 'They were taking them to be killed but they didn't give them water. So Cécile and I did.'

'What did Cécile's father have to say about that?'

Julia shrugged. 'He wasn't there. He was still inside at work.'

'Go and change.' She gave Julia a little push. 'Then come back and make the sticks.'

'I'll go if you tell me about the flower.'

'Julia. Enough. Flowers can curse.'

Julia was amazed. 'That flower? Anyway, how can flowers curse?'

'It's the spirit inside.'

'But how?' Julia persisted.

'You ask too many questions.'

'Oh, Thérèse.'

'*Non*. Go and change.' Thérèse began to sing very softly, one of the two Creole songs she was so fond of.

> '*Ai-o, p'end gar', p'end gar', p'end gar',*
> *Ai-o, p'end gar', ou a pa baisé mon pagai . . .*'

It was odd. The tune was merry and lively, yet the words threatened a beating. It made no sense.

Julia went indoors, through the pantry, into the dining room. The dining room opened out into the sitting room. At the far end was a curtain. Julia lifted it aside and went on through the hall to her bedroom, taking her tunic off over her head as she went.

A lot of things made no sense, and not just greegree, she thought. Only the week before, Noellie had taken one of her chickens from the run to kill for dinner. Julia had protested but it made no difference. She had watched the cook wring the chicken's neck but instead of dying and becoming limp and lifeless as she expected, it ran round and round the garden in circles, head lolling absurdly to one side. Julia's indignation had fled as she watched awestruck.

'It'll stop running soon,' Noellie said laconically, turning to go inside.

'But it's dead, Noellie. I saw you kill it,' Julia said.

'Ah *oui*, dead, not dead. It's all the same. I killed it. It'll stop running in a moment.' Then she had crossed herself as an afterthought. Nothing was ever quite as it seemed, Julia thought. Perhaps it was like the Resurrection. Jesus and everyone died and then came to life again, on the other side of some invisible line.

CHAPTER 9

'Like this: one, two, three, down; one, two, three, sideways!' Sister Dominic lifted her long habit and delicately kicked a foot out to the side. 'Is that clear?' Not waiting for their nods, she went on. 'I want you in two lines, men over here to my right, women there.'

The class shuffled into place. Julia, Marie and Cécile were men. Antoinette waved to them from the line of women on the other side of the stage. They were all supposed to be townspeople celebrating one of Joan of Arc's victories over the English.

'One, two, three, down!' Sister Dominic sang and Sister Agatha banged out the tune on the piano. The line of men hopped obediently behind her, winding in and out of the women's line. The more they did it, the easier it seemed and the more Julia began to enjoy herself.

'And now I'd like the heralds.'

The three of them stepped forward.

'Here.' Sister Dominic gave them each a stick. 'Your bugles will be ready tomorrow. You can use these for now. How are your costumes coming along? Cécile, yours is finished, I know.' In fact, she'd made it herself. Julia thought that might be because Cécile's parents were too poor to be able to buy the material.

'Mine's ready,' Julia said. She'd helped Thérèse make it the week before. She thought it was beautiful. It was a sky blue satin tunic reaching to just above the knee with orange fleurs-de-lys that her mother had painted on it. Her father had covered an old hat with velvet in the same blue and stuck a feather in it. Underneath that she had to wear blue tights.

'So's mine,' Marie said.

'Good. Bring them to the dress rehearsal next Tuesday. And now let's hear those lines. I want them said in one voice. Ready?'

Julia took a deep breath. She wanted to be word-perfect.

'Go.'

Sister Dominic conducted them.

'I have important news, my liege,' they said loudly, and again and a third time till the words came out as if from one mouth. On they went to their second line, until Sister Dominic was satisfied.

She clapped her hands to silence the class's murmurs. 'And now we'll do the scene where Saint Joan is going to be burned as a witch. Men and women: mingle.'

A witch, Julia thought. She put up her hand.

'Yes, Julia? What is it?' Sister Dominic stopped halfway across the stage.

'What's a witch?'

'Well Saint Joan wasn't one, even if the English said she was,' Sister Dominic answered obliquely, infuriating Julia.

'But what *is* a witch?' Julia tried again. She wanted to know *exactly*.

The nun looked hard at her and spoke carefully. 'A witch is someone who doesn't believe in God and who does the Devil's work.'

'What's "Devil's work"?'

'It means casting spells, making strange medicines that can kill people, and all sorts of other dangerous things,' Sister Agatha answered brusquely, getting up from the piano stool. 'Not the sort of things we want to think about. Now, where did you want the stake to be, Sister?'

Julia, rebuffed, bit her lip, thinking hard. 'Do you think the greegree man might be a kind of witch?' she whispered to Cécile.

Cécile looked startled. She shrugged. 'I don't know. Ssh. We're not meant to talk about it.'

'I know,' said Julia glumly.

Marie joined Julia in the queue for their lunch, chicken and plantains spooned out over steaming rice on enamel plates. Together they sat at one of the long tables in the communal eating hall. Cécile already had her lunch and had saved places for them. Little was heard above the scraping of spoons. The palm-leafed roof came low down the open sides of the hall and, as she ate, Julia gazed out through the fringe of leaves at the sky and the smaller classroom huts.

'Did you remember to ask your father?' she asked Cécile, quietly.

Cécile swallowed her mouthful before answering. 'Yes. He doesn't'.

'Doesn't what?' Marie asked inquisitively, over-hearing.

'Make candles,' Julia explained.

'Oh,' said Marie wisely, flicking her brown plaits over her shoulder the way she always did when she pretended she understood. Julia envied Marie her hair. It was so long she could sit on it.

Up on the high table, Mother Superior tinkled the silver bell at her elbow and stood. The girls rose, pushed in their chairs and waited.

'*Deo gratias*. Thanks be to God.'

'Amen,' they responded.

Chatter broke out at once. They had half an hour before they had to leave for the cathedral where once a week they went for mass; the rest of the afternoon was free. Julia and four others in the school didn't have to go because they were Protestant. But if you didn't go, you had to stay in an empty classroom doing home-work. She preferred to be with her friends.

She loved that solemn moment of entering the cath-edral after the chatter and hot sunshine outside. The Protestant church she went to with her parents and Thomas on Sunday was smaller but it too was always full. It was white-washed and purple bougainvillaea cascaded round the porch as you came in. This Catholic cathedral was starker and grander and filled with the smell of wax and incense that was steeped into the stone. Its strange sense of suspended mystery fas-cinated Julia.

81

At a signal they trooped forward. It was Julia's turn. The priest dipped his thumb into the silver platter held by the boy at his side. With one hand he brushed aside her fringe. With the other he pressed his thumb to her forehead twice in a cross. A cross of ashes. 'Dust thou art, to dust thou shalt return.' Burnt palm leaves . . . burning . . . fat . . . candles . . . She returned to her seat and knelt on the wooden kneeler next to Marie and rested her elbows on the back of the chair in front of her and folded her hands in prayer. Sister Dominic came to the empty chair on the other side of her in the aisle.

The priest intoned in Latin. When she tried only half listening, it didn't sound so very different from the chanting of the chaplain in English in her own church. She stood when the others stood, did what they did. The rituals had a sort of magic about them. They made the sign of the cross and so did she. They began to sing and the swell of their voices pleased her. They knelt again and she peeped as a bell rang once, twice. She watched the priest at the altar, gorgeous in purple vestment over white sleeves. He raised a silver chalice and sang words that she knew were about sacrifice. The chalice flashed in the light from six tall candles, as thick as her arm and longer, that stood on the altar. Each large candle must have been about the size of thirty of the small ones she and Thérèse had lit, she reckoned. She turned her head and looked behind her at the bank of small candles flickering bravely in the side altar, to check. Yes, thirty, she thought.

The priest began to speak to them. He reminded them that in Lent Jesus had been tempted in the desert. For forty days and forty nights he had withstood temptation. Now that it was Lent what were they going to sacrifice until Easter?

'Coca-Cola,' Marie whispered to Julia when she nudged her and asked.

'Honey,' said Cécile on Marie's other side.

Sister Dominic looked reprovingly at Julia for talking.

Marie waited until she was looking forward again.

'What about you?' she asked Julia, half under her breath.

Julia didn't answer. She didn't know. She wasn't even sure if Protestants gave up things for Lent.

'Thérèse,' she called as she rounded the end of the bungalow, home from school. 'Thérèse, are you there?' She heard a muffled call in answer. Thérèse was washing her hair under the outside tap at the large shallow sink near the chicken run. Julia stared, forgetting what she had needed Thérèse for. 'Why are you washing your hair now?'

'Because I've got the afternoon off, remember? I'm going to a wedding up there.' She jerked her head in the direction of the mountainside. 'Why haven't you changed?'

'I'm just going to. Whose wedding? May I come?'

'No. It's not for little English girls. *Allez*! Go and change.'

'Oh, Thérèse.'

Noellie shooed Julia away from the kitchen too. She looked hopelessly from Thérèse, the water splashing round her face, to Noellie, her great size blocking the kitchen door. Noellie didn't even relent and give her one of her biscuits when Julia tried smiling. She sighed and trailed off round to the front verandah. She knew she wasn't supposed to disturb the servants in the quiet of the afternoon, but just at the moment she didn't want to be on her own.

She thought she'd try Thomas. Occasionally when he came back from his school at the other end of Port Victoria they'd do things together.

Thomas was in his room, painting, concentrating hard and, sure enough, he ignored her when she came and hovered hopefully at his elbow. Eventually he said he wanted to finish his picture. Julia retreated to her own room. She flung off her uniform, pulled on shorts and a T-shirt and slouched outside, feeling fed up. She sat down with her back to the giant Dragon's Blood tree, careful not to lean back too hard. The tree bled real blood when you cut it. In the harbour below, the liner was preparing to sail. They were taking up the gangway that had been let down the side of the ship to the small boats.

A mosquito landed on her knee. She waited until it had gorged itself then brought the flat of her hand down on it sharply. The insect was too heavy and sluggish to rise and her blood burst from it, over the bite, preventing any itch. She examined the blood closely, the way it ran into her skin showing up tiny cracks. It looked unreal, not like her skin at all.

84

The whine of a car engine coming up the drive startled her. Her mother got out of the car and, spotting her, came over, looking flustered.

'Darling, we have to go out to tea and then to early dinner tonight. It's all rather last-minute. I'm going to change into another dress and meet Daddy at the Club. I'll have to ask Thérèse if she minds looking after you both after all.'

'She's going to a wedding,' Julia ventured, holding her breath.

'Perhaps she wouldn't mind taking you with her. I'll ask.' Julia crossed her fingers. She didn't think Thérèse would refuse her mother.

When her mother returned in a freshly ironed dress, her face clearer, she was smiling.

'That'll be all right, but you must dress smartly, both of you.'

Julia gave a little skip of happiness.

'And scrub that ink off your fingers,' her mother went on. Julia looked down at them ruefully. They were perpetually ink-stained from the dip pen she used at school, not very skilfully.

'What are you going to give up for Lent?' Julia asked her mother as she walked with her to the car.

Her mother shrugged. 'I hadn't thought about it. Why? Do you think I should give up something?'

'The priest said so today at mass. He said it should be a sacrifice. He said it had to be something we liked.'

'Then how about you giving up picking your mosquito bites,' her mother said, taking Julia's hand away from her face where it had been scratching, and getting into the driver's seat.

Julia pulled a face and closed the car door. Trust her mother to bring that up.

She watched the car go down the drive then ran to change into a dress and tell Thomas to dress up too. When they came out Thérèse was waiting for them, wearing ribbons in her hair and the dress she had just made, scarlet with great yellow flowers, She looked strangely sullen, almost uneasy, Julia thought. And Thomas was sulking; he hadn't wanted to leave his painting at all.

They walked slowly along the road, past scattered bungalows, down to the junction at the old French graveyard and then left up the hill. A little further and Thérèse nudged them off the road on to a path Julia had never noticed before. By now Thérèse was singing, solemn hymns mostly.

'This isn't the way to the cathedral, is it?' Thomas asked impatiently.

'*Non*.'

'No? Where are we going, Thérèse? You said a wedding.'

'Yes, a wedding. You'll see.'

She stopped, then turned and looked at them. 'Listen. This won't be a wedding like the one you went to last month in church,' she said. 'It'll be –' she hesitated '– different.' She frowned, then went on. 'And I don't think your parents would like to know about it either. Do you understand?'

Thomas and Julia exchanged glances.

'I wouldn't have brought you if I didn't have to. And I'll probably have to leave you on your own when we get there. Will you be all right?'

Thomas nodded. Julia's tummy did a nervous flip.

'Julia?'

'Yes,' she said, nodding too.

They walked on in single file down the narrow path. Palms and bushes and flowers flourished around them, blocking out the sun. Brightly coloured birds flew away from them as they approached. A green beetle crashed into Julia's cheek and she brushed it away. In the clearing ahead stood a house, long, low and wooden.

Thérèse smiled again at last. Briefly.

A crowd was jostling for position in front of the house, men in their best shorts and shirts, women in cotton frocks as brightly flowered as Thérèse's.

How odd, Julia thought, that there were no other children – at least, none that she could see. Palm wine was being poured liberally. Thérèse parked them on a rock at the edge of the clearing and went to fetch some. They saw her talking to a group of people, waving in their direction. Then she was back at their side, sipping the strong alcohol she never drank at home. She handed Julia and Thomas a large glass of coconut milk.

A man lurched past, hawking and spitting on the ground. Julia hastily moved her foot out of the way.

'You'll have to share the glass,' Thérèse said.

The music from the four musicians standing near the house was louder now. Thérèse shifted from one foot to the other. Her fingers twitched. She looked at the musicians and back at Thomas and Julia. 'Stay here,' she said, 'and be good. Please. I've told them you will be.' She almost said something else, but seemed to think better of it. She left their side.

People were starting to dance, slowly and solemnly, in circles that stayed tightly together and then intertwined in an intricate pattern. Julia and Thomas sat quietly, watching as the slow stately dancing gradually speeded up, getting faster and faster, until there was no stopping between dances, coloured dresses whirling, hats flying, Thérèse's face, a flash of yellow on her patterned scarlet dress. There was no one else there they recognized. Strange, Julia thought, how everyone looked so grave. People usually smiled when they danced, she thought. She turned to ask Thomas if he'd noticed but the blank, intent look on his face put her off and she stayed quiet.

The music went on and on, round and round. There seemed to be no beginning to it, and no end. No bird song broke its flow. There was only music, and feet stamping the ground.

Julia began to lose all sense of time. It was as if the dancers were in a great bubble and she and Thomas were just on the outside looking in. From somewhere inside the house came the thud of a drum; it grew louder, more insistent. It drowned the music and froze the dancers in their places. Its rhythms penetrated Julia's mind and pounded behind her eyes. She could hardly breathe.

Silence.

The drum had stopped. No one moved. And then

the unearthly shriek of a chicken, over and over again. A rhythmic, slow sighing, soft as the first pattern of rain, reached Julia. It grew to a murmur. It swelled to a chant, a torrent. One dancer detached himself from the crowd, and another, a third, a fourth . . . The scene tilted in front of Julia, bright greens and reds and purples and yellows spun and whirled into one. She felt clammy and cold. She wanted to be sick. She didn't understand what was going on. She put her hands over her ears and closed her eyes and wished it to go away.

Thérèse was shaking her. 'Come, Julia, time to go home.'

Dancers were twirling in the moonlight, musicians were still playing. Ordinary dancers, smiling, laughing, enjoying themselves. There were as many people in the clearing as there had been before but something had shifted. It all looked perfectly normal.

'But, Thérèse, the wedding?'

'It's over.'

'Over? Was I asleep, Thérèse? Where was the priest, Thérèse?' She looked round. 'Where's Thomas? What happened?' She clutched Thérèse, suddenly remembering the sensation of spinning into nothingness.

'Shhh. He's already gone home. He didn't enjoy it.'

'I thought I heard . . . I saw . . .'

'*Ou pas ne voir rien, ma p'tite, rien*. You saw nothing at all, little one. Come along.'

'Was that really a wedding party? Were they married earlier in the big cathedral?'

Thérèse looked away and nodded. 'That's right. And no more questions now, we're going home.'

In silence they walked back down the path and along the road, lit brightly by the moon and stars, Thérèse's arm round Julia's shoulders. It didn't seem so far coming home.

'Goodnight, Julia.'

'Goodnight.'

But once Julia reached her bedroom, she felt strange, too nervous to sleep alone. She crept into Thomas's bed, balancing on the hard edge beside him, scarcely daring to breathe.

He grunted and moved over. 'What do you want?'

'Why didn't you stay?'

'I got bored. All that funny greegree stuff, and you weren't watching anyway.'

'What greegree?'

'You know.'

'I don't. I was scared. What did you see?'

'Well not really anything, I suppose. I just thought, oh, I just wanted to come home. Good-night.' He twitched back into sleep before she was able to ask him any more.

In the night she half woke to feel herself being carried safely back to her own bed. Her father slid her in between the sheets and tucked her up.

'Did you enjoy yourself, poppet?' she heard him ask as if from a great distance.

She half tried to answer, but yawned instead and drifted off again.

CHAPTER 10

Julia climbed down from her tree. It was Saturday and Thomas had gone off sailing with Marcel. It was what he liked doing best. His boat was only big enough for two and she wasn't invited. Her parents had left for the office. She wandered to the back of the house, calling, 'Thérèse-o!'

'She's gone to see her sister.' Fat Noellie came out of the kitchen, her faded frock glued darkly to her waist and armpits. 'I've just made some flapjacks. They're still warm. Like one?'

'Yes please!' Julia followed her eagerly into the kitchen and dipped a hot crumbly biscuit into the pot of melted chocolate. Noellie sat down and patted her lap. Julia went over and subsided on to the great thighs. Such moments were precious. Usually Noellie was too busy and had no time for her. Not today. She began singing, her voice sinking to a hum, rising to a croon, swelling to a full-bellied roar, sinking again, up and down. Julia closed her eyes and leaned back, enjoying the motion. It stopped. She willed it to go on but it didn't.

'Off,' Noellie said firmly. 'I have work to do. Why don't you go and play?'

'I want to go across to Beau Vallon and swim.'

Noellie held out another flapjack and didn't answer. Julia held her breath. She knew she was perfectly safe going across the island on her own; she had done it before. She knew the path.

'*Bien*. All right. Leave a note on the table for Maman and Papa. But go and brush your teeth first.'

'OK.' Julia ran through to her bedroom. A moment later, swimming costume crumpled in one hand, she set off barefoot down the drive.

Half an hour later, the path emerged on to a dirt road. Julia crossed it and broke through bushes to the white sand and water's edge. Ahead of her the sea glittered as far as the horizon, interrupted only by Silhouette, an island outlined against the sky. The bay curved round in a wide arc, empty of life. She went down to the water and walked along the surf, toes digging into the soft sand.

A dark shape detached itself from the shadows of the bushes. It was Pa'tout, the black, half-blind stray dog who commandeered the beach at Beau Vallon, attaching himself sycophantically to the first person who came along. He tagged along in front of her, sidling just ahead of her feet, forcing Julia to go further into the water in order not to have to keep changing step.

Halfway along the beach she left the water and headed for the thick softer sand again, crossed the road and walked down a drive to the hotel where Marie lived. Her parents owned the hotel, one of only two on the island. It sprawled along the sea, a collection of tiny granite houses, each with its own shower and verandah, palm-leafed roof blending with the coconut palms above.

Marie was at the back, spooning out a custard-apple.

'Hello.' Julia sat down on the ground beside her.

'Oh, hello.' Marie looked more pleased to see her than she sounded. She finished her custard-apple then put the skin and spoon on the ground and licked her fingers very carefully, one by one. By the time she had finished licking, the ants were gathering to feast on the skin. 'I've got something to show you,' she said mysteriously. 'It's a secret.'

Julia looked up from watching the ants. 'What?'

Marie put a finger to her lips and got up, beckoning.

They tiptoed across the grassy yard to a small narrow room, one of a row on the other side. It had a door but no window, just a wide gap between its low roof and the wooden wall. Marie fetched two boxes and motioned Julia on to one of them.

Standing on the boxes, their eyes just reached the gap. Inside, Rose, one of the younger maids at the hotel, was on the bed with a man. Intent on what they were doing, they didn't notice the girls whose eyes were glued to them. Until Marie sniggered.

Rose shot up. She grabbed a potty at the side of the bed. Julia and Marie leaped off their boxes. They weren't fast enough. The brimming yellow contents of the potty came flying out through the gap and fell on them in a smelly shower.

'Ugh!' Julia spluttered, shaking her head like a dog.

Marie, running away, turned, giggling. 'Come *on*, Julia,' she urged.

They didn't stop running till they reached the beach and the sea where they splashed themselves clean, breathless from running and giggling.

'Her *face*!' Julia gasped.

'We'll be able to tease her now, won't we?' laughed Marie. 'And she always said she hadn't got a boy-friend!'

'All the same,' Marie went on, sobering slightly. 'We'd better stay out of her way for this afternoon.'

Julia nodded. 'Race you to the rocks then!' and she was off, but she didn't have much puff left and they soon slowed to walk the last bit, their T-shirts and hair drying in the sun.

Julia heard a soft snuffling and turned to see Pa'tout again. He halted and cowered, pathetically wagging his fat stumpy tail.

'Go away, Pa'tout, go on!' Marie shouted crossly at him.

His tail faltered but he stood his ground, avoiding their eyes.

'Oh leave him, Marie. It's his beach.'

'No it isn't. Anyway, he stinks.'

Julia shrugged and walked on. Marie followed. Pa'tout trailed behind.

'Are you staying tonight?'

'I haven't asked,' Julia said. 'I'd like to.'

The tide was well in when they reached the point of the bay, the sea swirling around the huge boulders scattered here, maybe from the time that the mountains

94

had been volcanoes, Julia's father had once told her. In Gondwanaland days, she added to herself. Her favourite boulder was down a channel and at high tide it became its own little island as it was now. She and Marie splashed towards it, leaving Pa'tout whining miserably at the water's edge. When he saw that they weren't coming for him, his head dropped and he turned and lumbered off, looking for someone else to attach himself to.

They clambered up the rock, finding familiar footholds in the granite. It was full of hollows and valleys and they climbed into one particularly scooped-out bowl where they kept a collection of cowries of every size: small blonde shells no bigger than Julia's little finger; large gleaming tortoiseshell ones the size of her fist.

'There. That was my secret,' Marie said, sitting down and taking the cowries out of the corner and beginning to arrange them. 'Now it's your turn. What's your secret?'

The Hill came jumping back into Julia's head.

'I can't,' she said, her voice low.

'Why not?' Marie demanded.

'Because – because I promised not to.'

'Who did you promise?' Marie sat back on her heels, watching her.

Julia looked away from the delicate patterns they had been making with the shells and gazed out to sea, all the laughter from spying on Rose forgotten now. On the surface all you could see was water, but not far out, where there was a line of breakers, was the reef.

They had been out there with Marie's father only the week before, wearing rubber flippers, goggles and snorkels. Underneath the sea had been vivid red, white and green coral palaces which reached up through the water and almost scraped their tummies as they floated above. Through the palace doors, jewelled fish of every shape and size darted and glided, in ones and twos and swarming shoals. From here, looking at the water and breakers, you would never guess at that other world, she thought, you would never know that it existed.

'Who?' persisted Marie.

'Thérèse.' Julia turned back to meet Marie's gaze. 'I really can't say. It's – important. I wish –'

'But I'm your friend.' Marie's lips were beginning to pout in a sulk.

'I know,' Julia agreed. The sun was hot beneath her on the stone. Perhaps she could tell Marie about the wedding, she thought suddenly. Thérèse hadn't actually said she couldn't, only that her parents weren't to know. 'I could tell you another secret,' she offered.

'A second-best secret?' Marie considered. 'OK.'

'We went to a wedding yesterday, Thomas and me –'

'Weddings are boring,' Marie said scornfully.

'Not this one –' Julia began to protest but Marie had her hand up.

'Listen,' she said.

There it came again, the call of a conch shell, low and clear, three times.

'Fish! They're pulling in the fish! Come on.' They scrambled down the boulder. They rounded it and saw a semicircle of men waist high in the sea, slowly wading in to shore.

By the time they reached the fishermen a small knot of onlookers had gathered. Slowly the semicircle closed and moved out of the water, the men drawing the net they held between them tighter, causing panic among the thrashing fish trapped inside. The two men at either end of the net moved further up the beach, dragging the net over their shoulders, followed by the others, their darned shorts wet from the salt water. The red, blue and silver fish now exposed to the air jumped and struggled. Julia squatted on the warm sand, Marie at her side, and watched the men sort the catch, deftly taking them from the flapping heap and tossing mackerel in one basket, capitain rouge and parrot fish in another, bourgeois in a third. Pa'tout squeezed through the small group and sniffed at the bourgeois, slavering. A fisherman chased him away, a fish brandished in his hand. Pa'tout made a wide circle then smarmed his way back to the girls, seeking comfort. But they ignored him. If she stayed the night, Julia thought, they would have fresh fish for dinner, curried. Her mouth watered in anticipation.

Marie's mother was coming out of the main hotel building as they walked back, her hair brushed out from her head in a mass of curls which the sun shone through. She bent down. 'Hello Julia,' she said, lips lightly brushing her cheek, just long enough for Julia to catch sight through the open neck of the shirt of small breasts uncovered by any bra. 'Will you be staying the night?'

Julia nodded shyly. 'Yes please. But I haven't asked my parents yet.' Marie's mother made her shy. She wasn't usually much of a hugger or a kisser. In fact, Julia never felt she was much like a mother at all, partly because of things like no bra, and never wearing skirts, or almost never. The light kiss had surprised her.

'Good.' The woman straightened, lips pursed, and took a puff of the cigarette in the long tortoiseshell holder that she'd kept out at right angles to her body. She always had a cigarette in her hand. It seemed to be an extension of her arm. 'I'm going into town later on,' she went on, 'so I'll pop in and tell your parents you'll be here, shall I, mmm? And I'll bring Thomas back with me if he'd like to come.' She brushed sand from Marie's arm and drifted back inside, not waiting for their answer.

'Come on,' Marie said. 'Let's have a Coke.'

They went to the bar at the end of the verandah, perched on high cane stools and asked the barman for Coca-Colas. 'Without a straw, please,' Julia added. She adored the sweet brown stuff but her parents wouldn't let her have it at home, except as a special treat.

The barman set the tall glasses down in front of them and took two chocolate biscuits from a screw-top jar and added them for good measure.

'Thank you,' Julia said, unwrapping the silver paper

and biting. She waited for her glass to frost over from the cold of the ice inside, then gulped greedily. She looked sideways at Marie and watched her swallow. 'Hey!' she exclaimed, remembering. 'You said you were going to give up Coke for Lent!'

Marie put the glass down quickly. 'Bother. I'd forgotten.' She sipped more delicately. 'Then I'll give up chocolate instead.' She passed Julia the remaining half of her biscuit. Julia ate it quickly before she changed her mind. She wasn't at all sure that she believed Marie.

Marie's father appeared behind them. He put his arms round them. 'Your sister was looking for you,' he said. 'She's gone swimming. And it's time you left this bar. You know the rules.'

The rules were only one Coke in the afternoon and that they weren't to hang around the verandah once the hotel guests arrived as they were now doing, in dribs and drabs, pulling out the cane chairs and sitting in small groups.

'Here, take some sandwiches.' He piled some on a plate and gave them to Julia. 'And now, scram!' he said, a little more fiercely, lightly tweaking Julia's ear.

Without any discussion they went to change into bathing costumes and in no time they were running across the plantation, among the scattered bungalows of the hotel and out on to the beach. Anne, Marie's older sister, was already there, halfway to the raft that was moored in the bay. Marie plunged through the waves, her plaits streaming out behind her. Julia,

bearing the plate of sandwiches, had to be more careful. She walked in as far as she could, lifting her feet
high in the swirling water, then she turned on her back
and began awkwardly to swim, keeping the plate out
of the water, trying not to let it get splashed.

She trod water when she finally reached the raft
while Marie reached down and took the sandwiches
from her. She hauled herself out of the water and on to
the bamboo slats, avoiding the sharp shells stuck to
the oil drums that kept it afloat.

'Watch out!' Anne said crossly. 'You're tipping the
raft over.'

Julia and Marie ignored her complaints.

'Would you like a sandwich?' Julia said sweetly,
holding them out.

Mollified, Anne took one.

Julia and Marie lay on their tummies, heads hanging
over the edge, munching, while Anne gazed up at the
sky on the other side of the raft. Julia loved feeling the
gentle swell of the sea rocking them. Striped parrot
fish darted about beneath them, in and out of the trails
of pale green seaweed that were attached to the bottom of the raft. To her relief, Marie seemed to have
forgotten that she owed her a secret.

They put out their fingers and the fish nibbled at
them with soft, sucking lips. Julia dropped crumbs on
to the surface one by one and they rushed at them, a
mass of yellow, red and black. The sun bounced and
shimmered on the water and Julia felt she could stay
like this for ever.

By the time Thomas arrived and swam out to join

them, they were playing around the raft, diving from it and scattering the fish while they swam on down and down through the clear turquoise water till they reached the sand on the bottom and picked a handful to bring up to the raft, ears singing from holding their breath.

Changing for bed that night they heard a faint sound of music that wasn't jazz or love songs from the gramophone. They crept round past the kitchens and reached the hibiscus bushes at the side of the dining room and stopped there in the shadows. The dining room was a square building, a little raised up, with low stone walls and open sides. Standing on the edge of the light that splashed out from it on to the grass were four musicians, playing traditional Seychellois music. Up in the dining room, a waiter poured wine and Rose collected plates. People were listening, but they were only being polite. Julia could tell from the stiff way their heads were turned to the men. The music went on and on, a grave monotonous melody.

Inside the dining room a man began to clap, very slowly. The musicians bowed with dignity and did not stop their playing. Now other guests were joining in, clap, clap, clap, slowly, till the sound was competing with the music. The musicians, bewildered, faltered. One of them, looking up puzzled, caught sight of the four children at his side. His eyes rested on Julia.

'Thomas!' she whispered in alarm, grabbing his arm. 'It's the musicians from that wedding.'

He tensed and looked too. 'Yes,' he said.

'They mustn't clap them like that,' Julia said passionately to Marie. 'Can't you tell your father to tell them to stop?' She was talking in her normal voice; the applause was so loud now that she didn't need to keep her voice down.

Marie tried, waving to her father.

He came over, irritated. 'What are you doing out here? You should be in bed. Go on. I'll come over and say goodnight in a moment,' and he hustled them away.

As they went, Julia looked back over her shoulder and saw him paying one of the musicians, who bowed his head over the money. The others were silently, slowly putting away their instruments in the shadows, ignored by the chattering, brightly lit diners. She felt ashamed for the diners.

Segregation at bedtime was strict; Julia shared Marie and Anne's bedroom and Thomas had his own smaller room. But once Marie and Anne's father and then their mother had been to say good-night, they smuggled Thomas into the cupboard which stood in the corner of the girls' room. He agreed he would wake them in the middle of the night so that they could go to watch the sea.

Instead it was Julia who stayed awake, listening to the sounds of music and laughter dim and die away, to the clatter of dishes and chatter in the kitchen fade, till all she could hear was the faint whisper of the sea. When she was sure all had settled for the night, she waited expectantly for Thomas to come and wake her, but even in their room all was still. Eventually, tense with impatience, she kicked off her sheet and leaned across first to the right, then to the left to shake Marie and Anne awake.

'It's *time*,' she hissed. She tiptoed over to the cupboard and opened it. She prodded her brother where he lay on a shelf. Prodded him again. 'You forgot to wake us up,' she whispered.

'Leave me alone,' he said crossly. She sighed, and poked him in a different spot. He only curled up more tightly, just like a centipede.

'Won't he wake up?' Anne was peering at him too.

'No.' She examined him. Marie slipped under her arm and began tickling Thomas. He struggled away from her searching fingers, giggling.

'Sshh!' Marie chided him, not stopping.

'All right!' he gasped, banging his head on the shelf above. 'I'll come.'

The four of them stepped cautiously out on the grass and paused in case anyone was there to see them and send them back to bed. There was no one. They walked round the end of the main building and past the verandah. The coral creeper falling over it looked like myriads of silver caterpillars in the moonlight, Julia thought. When she looked up at the sky, she saw that it was thick with stars, like a cloud.

They walked warily down through the trees and bungalows, etched sharply against the light; their colour washed from them, they were mysterious night versions of their daily selves. A sudden gust of wind rattled the palm leaves, responding to the pounding of the surf beyond.

The beach was cooler in the dark and felt damp under Julia's feet. Behind them, the darker trees and sleeping hotel. Ahead of them, no sound but that of the waves hitting the beach and pulling back, hitting and pulling back, each time trying to take the sand with them.

In silence they faced the water, watching in awe what they had come to see. When the waves hit the beach they exploded into dancing silver as if every drop contained a fairy-sized lantern.

Julia sat down to stare at the silver fire. Someone sat beside her. She didn't turn to look, absorbed by the phosphorescence, as she'd been told it was called. It was caused by millions of tiny worms. But knowing that didn't make it any less magical.

'Marcel's asked me to go to Grand' Anse with him for his birthday. On Wednesday.' It was Thomas.

Her head swung round to him, away from the glowing, shimmering silver. 'Can I come too?' she asked eagerly.

'No. It's his birthday, I just said so. He hasn't invited you. We're going with his parents,' he added unnecessarily.

'Oh.' Her voice sounded flat. She looked back at the sea, scrunching sand with her toes. 'That's the day before our school play,' she said.

Thomas ignored her interruption. 'We've got this plan,' he went on. 'It's only right you should know about it. Only you mustn't tell anyone. Promise?'

'I promise,' she said.

'You've got to mean it,' he said fiercely. 'You're always blurting things out.'

'I promise,' she repeated. 'You can trust me. Really.' After all, she hadn't told anyone about going up The Hill. Except Thérèse.

'What plan?' Marie asked, coming closer and over-hearing.

Thomas didn't answer her. Marie shrugged and moved on down to the water and began to paddle at the edge. Now there was a sprinkling of silver lights on her ankles.

'It's Marcel's plan really,' he went on in a quieter whisper to Julia. 'We're going to take a lilo and –'

'A lilo!' Julia gasped, 'at Grand' Anse! You can't!'

'Yes we can,' he contradicted her.

'But it's forbidden.' Her face puckered in distress.

'We're not allowed to *play* on a lilo is all.' Thomas's chin pointed firmly upwards. 'Well, we're not going to. Anyway, listen. Our plan is to use it as a boat to get round to the treasure man's beach. We want to see if we can approach it from the sea and surprise him. We want to see more treasure, not just a doll.'

'There isn't any. Everyone says so.'

'We don't know that for sure, do we?' he answered. 'I don't think anyone ever asks him.'

'But what if he sees you coming?' Her fingers had found a new mosquito bite and were scratching feverishly.

'He won't.' Thomas said with confidence. 'He won't be expecting anyone to be coming from the sea. It's the

105

wrong direction. I reckon that–' His voice trailed away as Marie joined them again.

'What are you two talking about?' she asked. 'Is it another secret?'

'No,' said Thomas quickly, 'not at all.'

'Oh.' She yawned. 'Let's go back to bed. I'm tired.'

Her yawn spread, first to Julia and then to Thomas.

'All right.' The yawn spread to Anne, who laughed and began to walk away.

They all got up and turned their backs on the sea, Thomas bringing up the rear.

Julia slipped back until she was walking alongside him. 'Don't,' she pleaded. There were butterflies in her tummy.

'It's all right. He won't do anything to us,' Thomas whispered back. 'Anyway, we're going.'

But it wasn't the treasure man Julia was scared of, was the lilo, it was dangerous. Don't take it, she wanted to say, the lilo's dangerous, things aren't right. But the words stayed in the back of her throat.

'Remember you promised,' Thomas said.

She nodded unhappily.

CHAPTER 11

Julia's mother came to fetch them early the next afternoon.

'Daddy's finally got the badminton net out of the box,' she told them, 'and he's already painted the lines on the court. We thought we'd christen it this afternoon.' She moved down into second gear and swung the car round Banana Bend.

Julia cannoned across the back seat into Thomas. 'May we all play?' she asked, righting herself.

'Yes, darling,' her mother answered, braking hard to avoid a chicken. Julia banged hard into the front seat. 'Sorry. Anyway, yes. And we've asked Brother Joseph and Brother André to come and play too.'

'Brother André,' Thomas said gloomily from his corner. Brother André tried to teach him geometry at school. Thomas wasn't much good at it.

'He'll be all right,' their mother said reassuringly. Just then she tooted the horn as they turned into the drive and saw ahead of them two monks on bicycles, their long white habits flapping out on either side of the wheels.

They crawled up the drive behind them and Julia was out of the car the minute they reached the top. 'Brother Joseph!' she exclaimed with delight. Ever since he had spent one whole afternoon teaching her to play table tennis and telling her shaggy dog stories he had been a firm favourite.

Thomas followed rather more slowly. He shook his teachers' hands politely and escorted them to the badminton court, subdued at having them there.

But by the time they had played a couple of games, Thomas was flushed and smiling. They played in different combinations before ending with Julia and the two monks on one side playing against Thomas and their parents on the other.

Brother André and Brother Joseph hoisted up their robes and exposed white-clad calves before thwacking the funny feathered shuttlecock back to the other side, Brother Joseph hooting with laughter. 'My robe got in the way!' he shouted, each time he missed.

'Why not take it off?' Julia suggested, hoping that he would, curious to see what exactly monks wore underneath.

'You'd all have a fit!' he answered.

'Not to mention the Bishop,' Brother André said drily. 'I expect he'd report you to the Pope.'

'Oh.' Julia's eyes widened. 'How terrible,' she said sympathetically, and missed the shuttlecock as it came flying back over the net at her.

They stopped for long cold drinks of lime juice.

Julia's mother shook the bottle at her. 'It's empty. Would you go and get another bottle from the fridge, darling?'

Julia nodded. She hummed as she crossed the dining-room floor to the pantry for the gin bottle where they kept their boiled water.

The earth lurched.

Her feet stopped, rooted to the spot. The humming died on her lips. Through the French windows ahead of her the trees and the outline of St Anne sharpened against the sky. The silence around her was sharp, intense. All birds, crickets, voices were stilled. Julia felt alone on the earth and the world just beginning. She swung her head round and saw her parents, Thomas, Brother Joseph and Brother André frozen in a tableau, hands tightly round their glasses of lime juice. The Hill was framed behind them.

Another mighty lurch and a trembling.

Julia closed her eyes.

When she opened them again, the birds were singing and the voices of Thomas and Brother Joseph were raised excitedly.

Her mother ran to her. 'It's all right, darling,' she said, cuddling her. 'It must have been an earth tremor.' Julia could hear the shake in her mother's voice though and knew that she had been scared too.

She stared at The Hill and wondered what she and Thomas had awakened. It wasn't all right, she thought suddenly. Everything wasn't all right at all.

But the feeling left almost as swiftly as it had come. They went back to their game of badminton, their laughter a little louder than before the tremor, their game a little jollier.

Later, when the brothers had left for chapel and they had had tea, Julia sat at the Dragon's Blood tree,

Simba flopped at her side. A few yards away her father was working on a painting of the harbour below. He had started it just after her last birthday and it was now two months before her next. He said he didn't mind it taking a long time. Julia did. She wanted to see what it would look like finished.

'You two will have to eat on your own tonight,' Julia's mother said, coming over and handing her father a beer. 'And we should get changed, Will.'

Julia had forgotten that her parents were having guests to dinner. 'Can we stay up?'

'No,' her father answered, putting away his brushes and folding up the easel.

Julia didn't try pleading. She wasn't surprised. She always asked. One day, she knew, the answer would be yes. 'What are Thomas and I going to have for dinner?' she asked instead.

'Sardines on toast.'

Julia was pleased. It was one of her favourite dishes.

'And green beans,' her mother added. 'And banana whip flan afterwards. Now go and wash and put on your nightgown.'

'But it's still light,' she protested indignantly.

'I know. Not for much longer though, and I don't want any last-minute rush. Will you tell Thomas?'

Julia dawdled in her room, rearranging her books in alphabetical order on the shelves. Some of the covers were partly eaten away by white ants.

'Julia,' her mother warned, standing at the door in her dressing gown. 'Come on, sweetheart. I don't want to have to tell you again.'

She scrambled to her feet. Outside, the sky was turning from deep orange to vivid purple as the sun went down behind The Hill. 'We're going to have sardines on toast and banana whip flan,' she told Thomas in his room. 'And we're to get into our night-clothes now. Hurry up!' she added, in case he hadn't heard.

By the time they were at table it was dark outside and there were candles lit on the table.

As they ate, Julia's father appeared, changed into formal clothes for dinner. His shoes were black and shiny and he was smart in his white mess jacket cut high and sharp above the black cummerbund and trousers. He took the gramophone out of a cupboard, selected a record and put it on. Julia licked the last of the banana off her spoon and slid off the chair and stood beside him, watching.

Her mother came out in a long dress, deep blue and softly clinging.

'Thank you, Thérèse,' she said as Thérèse cleared the table. 'I think we'll have the candles tonight too.'

Julia had already blown them out. The smell of burning wax still hung in the air. She ran for the box of matches but Thomas had got there first. They struggled briefly over who should light the candles. Thomas won, but magnanimously passed Julia the matches to light most of the second candlestick. When all six candles were burning, they turned around and watched their mother in their father's arms dancing in great sweeps round the room. Julia thought they looked beautiful. When the music stopped they rested in each other's arms for a moment. Then they smiled and broke away.

'May I have the pleasure of the next dance, poppet?' Julia's father bowed to her.

She smoothed her nightdress and held out her arms as her mother had done. Her father whirled her solemnly over the polished floor of the sitting room as the voice on the record crooned. Round and round she went, spinning like a top, one two three, one two three. In the corner of her eye she saw her mother teaching Thomas the steps. She didn't need to learn, not if she was dancing with her father; he made it seem so natural and easy.

They heard the sound of car doors being slammed and Simba barking.

'Bed,' their mother said, opening a French window to go out and meet the guests. 'Goodnight,' and kissed them. 'I'll look in on you later.'

Thomas stopped at her door. 'Play Racing Demons?' he suggested.

She beamed. They found two packs of cards in her games box, shuffled, cut, exchanged packs, 'Ready, steady, go!' and laid them out, four single cards upwards and thirteen demons on the side.

It was a game they often played, sometimes with their parents, and they were quick at it. Thomas was a steady player; Julia was more erratic.

This time she reached a hundred first.

'Well done,' Thomas said generously, green eyes smiling at her.

'Another game?' Julia suggested, starting to shuffle the cards again.

'Or let's watch?' He jerked his head in the direction of her cupboards.

'OK.'

They opened the tall cupboard doors that lined one wall of her room and climbed up the shelves to the top. There was just room in the gap between the cupboards and the ceiling to lie down and look through the grating set high in the wall. They peered down into the sitting room to watch the guests and tried to eavesdrop.

But the conversation was uninteresting and Julia began to get sleepy. 'I'm going down,' she told Thomas, and by the time she was settling in bed he was climbing down too. She didn't bother to draw the curtains.

'Good-night,' he said.

''night.'

She drifted back to the surface a little later, heard faint voices and the clinking of cutlery coming through from the dining room, and went back to sleep.

Up on The Hill something was stirring. A small brown cloud detached itself from the dark trees and moved across the shallow valley. It headed for the open window and flew in.

In Julia's dream she thought a mosquito net was brushing across her face. She felt a tickling on her arms where they lay flung outside the sheet. She shifted her head on the pillow and something crawled across her

113

cheek and down to her ear. Half-waking, she realized that the tickling was real. It was quiet in the house; the guests must have gone and her parents must be in bed. She felt more feet crawling, antennae probing, on her eyelids, across her hand. The same crawling, tickling was down her arm and under her armpit. She kept her eyes closed. She imagined she was at the top of the cupboard looking down at herself. She froze. She didn't dare breathe. There was a heaving mass of insects on top of her; they were as long as her middle finger and thick, their wings hard and gleaming. She thought she would sink, fouled, under the multitude of insects. Perhaps, if she tried hard enough to pretend they weren't there, they would go away, fly back through the open window the way they must have come, back up to The Hill. They didn't. The blood surged to her head, she wanted to shout for help but no sound would come. She felt a flickering across her lips, a crawling at her ears. Her horror drove her out of bed at last and she ran, beating her body with her hands, shaking her head free, mouth open in terror, feet squashing giant beetles as they fell, ran in terror to her parents' room. 'Cockroaches!' she screamed, sobbing. Her mother lifted the sheet and took her into bed and cuddled her back to sleep.

In the morning the cloud of cockroaches had gone, flown back through the open window, leaving behind the few she had trodden on as proof that she hadn't imagined them: large, brown squashed beetles. She took her sandal and pushed them together in a small pile, a nerve in her bottom lip jumping and quivering. She turned her back on them so that she couldn't see them, and got dressed for school.

CHAPTER 12

'I'm going to the Gardens,' Cécile said, as they went out of the school gate, later than usual because of the dress rehearsal for the play. 'Do you want to come?'

Julia stopped suddenly and another girl bumped into her. All through the play she had forgotten about Thomas and his plan. Now she remembered again. 'Thomas is off to Grand' Anse,' she said, ignoring the other girl who was tut-tutting at her.

Cécile waited for more but none came. 'So?' she asked.

'It's dangerous.' Julia took off her hat and crumpled up the rim in her hand. She heard the plaited straw crack where it bent.

'I know that,' Cécile said impatiently. 'Last year when we went over to Praslin to see Tante Marie I was sick all day in the boat, the sea was so rough. Anyway, are you coming to the Gardens?'

Julia shuffled her feet. 'You don't understand. He's going on a lilo. It's forbidden.' She was unable to say more. Another promise.

Cécile was already walking away from her. 'Oh come on if you're coming. We can ride the tortoises.'

The giant land tortoises intrigued Julia. Most of them were at least one hundred years old. Older than her grandfather. She darted after Cécile, swerving to avoid a bicycle that came bearing down on her.

The Botanical Gardens had lawns cut so short you'd think they'd been shaved. The grass was as smooth as green silk, and it didn't itch like the grass at home. They headed for the giant land tortoises' enclosure and sat on the grass outside to watch them.

In fact there wasn't much to see. Six or seven tortoises were in the corner in the shade of a tree, huddled up, heads and legs tucked in, their shells overlapping. They looked just like a pile of rocks.

'Cécile,' Julia asked, watching one of the rocks shift and settle again. 'Have you really given up honey for Lent?'

'Of course,' Cécile said.

'Really and truly?' Julia persisted. 'Marie said she'd give up Coca-Cola but she didn't. Now she says she'll give up chocolate.'

'Well that's Marie,' Cécile sounded scornful. 'Once you say you'll give up something you have to. Everyone knows that.'

'What has your father given up?'

Cécile waved a hand vaguely in the air. 'Smoking. I think. Something anyway. Last year it was yams, and he loves yams. Let's stir up the tortoises,' and she was over the fence approaching them.

Julia joined her, not wanting to be left out. She knocked lightly on one shell. The tortoise stirred grumpily, stretched out its funny prehistoric neck, stared at nothing in particular, blinked and retreated once more. Julia tore up a handful of grass from beneath the tree and scratched the underside of the shell with the nails of her other hand. The head began to emerge once more. Julia proferred the grass. The tortoise rolled off the huddle of shells and lumbered after her as she retreated a few steps before giving him some. The top of his shell came up to her knees. The grass seemed to give him energy and he began to move almost perkily. Quickly she climbed on to him and sat astride as he rocked his slow way across the grass. But it was a disappointingly short ride. As soon as he reached the shade of a tree in the opposite corner, he stopped.

'Come on,' she cajoled him, leaning forward to speak to his head. 'Don't stop yet.' But it was no good.

She didn't get off straightaway just in case he moved again. Perched on the shell, she wondered again about Lent. She didn't really see the point in Cécile giving up honey for forty days. What good did it do anyone? Surely, there was no point in giving something up unless it helped someone. If she ever gave up something, she resolved, it would have to be important and it would help. It would really be a sacrifice. Cheered at having sorted that out, she looked across at Cécile. Her tortoise had come to a standstill too.

'Do you want to come home with me and play?' Julia asked.

Cécile shook her head. 'I can't. I've got to go back and look after Daniel and Gaetanne.'

Disappointment settled on Julia. She didn't want

Cécile to go. Nor did she want to go with her; she'd rather be at home, only not just yet. She wanted to delay going home. She didn't know why.

Something flickered at the edge of the tortoise's shell and caught her eye. A cockroach edged into sight, brown, glossy, foul. It twitched its long antennae in her direction.

It knew she was here, Julia thought dully. It was searching her out. She shuddered. The nerve in her bottom lip jumped in time to the cockroach's twitching. She whimpered, not able to help herself.

She leapt off the tortoise, climbed the fence and left the enclosure, not looking back. She stood on the grass on the other side and shook her head to clear it of the muzzy buzzing there, trying not to cry.

'Please stay just five minutes more,' she pleaded with Cécile, now at her side and looking surprised.

'All right,' her friend said. 'We'll go out the long way round.'

They went out the very long way round, dawdling across lawns and down paths drenched in sweetness from the frangipani trees to a shaded part of the gardens where a group of palm trees grew high above their heads.

Cécile stopped at one and patted its trunk.

'This,' she said.

'This?' Julia echoed. 'What about it? It's a coco-de-mer tree.' They had a coco-de-mer shell at home, polished. It looked just like somebody's bottom. They kept guavas and oranges and bananas in it.

'When I was in Praslin,' Cécile said, 'Tante Marie

118

took me to the Vallée de Mai where there are lots and lots of coco-de-mer trees like this. It was really dark in the valley. She said—' Cécile broke off and looked around to make sure no one was listening – 'she said that at night-time they make love.'

'They make love?' Julia repeated incredulously, staring up at the tree. 'How can they? They're just trees.'

'They're not just trees. There's a male tree and a female tree and they do it together at night.'

They both looked up.

'This one's male. Look—' and Cécile pointed upwards.

Julia was impressed. She tried to imagine the tops of trees bending towards each other in the wind. 'Have you seen them do it?' she asked, becoming a little less sceptical.

'Of course not. They do it at night. Everybody knows that. And you mustn't disturb them. No one walks through the Vallée after sunset.'

'If you did, what would happen?' Julia wanted to know. 'Would you be cursed?' The feeling of dread was back.

Cécile was already wandering away.

'Oh, I expect so,' she said.

On the other side of the island, Marcel was squatting on the sand, blowing hard into a green lilo, inflating it.

'Whew.' He put his thumb over the nozzle, brushed a hand across his mouth and passed it to Thomas. 'Your turn.'

Thomas took it willingly and blew till the rubber mattress was hard and bouncy.

They carried it into the sea and lay on it in turns, hooting with laughter as the waves tipped them first one way then another. Marcel's parents were watching them from the beach. Thomas went tumbling off it in one wave and felt the undertow pull him down. He came up gasping and chortling, spitting out water with the sand churned up in it. The lilo was just ahead of him, bobbing in a wave, and he caught it. Marcel swam out to him. They were close now to the outer line of breakers. The sea the other side looked relatively calm and smooth. Another wave swept past, lifting them as they held on to the lilo with their hands and taking them further out. On the beach they could see Marcel's parents now deep in conversation.

'Shall we?' Thomas asked Marcel.

Marcel nodded, his eyes glinting with excitement.

They heaved themselves on to the lilo so that they were lying across it, side by side, leaving their arms and legs free to manoeuvre. 'It should be easy enough to get round to the bay from here,' Thomas said. 'And the treasure man will never expect us.'

Another wave came and they were pulled out to sea in the powerful undertow, into the smooth sea beyond. They paddled hard with their arms now, kicking out with their legs at the same time. The lilo began to move swiftly, propelled by an invisible force beneath the waters.

There was a shout from the beach as Marcel's parents saw them carried out over the line of breakers. Marcel's father was on his feet now, waving and yelling for them to come back. Thomas waved back reassuringly but as he did so he couldn't help noticing how quickly Marcel's father seemed to be moving to the left of them. The current was bearing them away even more rapidly than they had expected, and in the wrong direction, not to the right, not towards the treasure man but away from him. Desperately he tried to slow down the lilo.

'Paddle!' Marcel said fiercely.

'I am!' Thomas retorted through gritted teeth. He was scared. This wasn't at all how they'd planned it.

'Get off!' Marcel cried. 'Thomas! Get off!' and he slipped away. Thomas twisted round to look, unsure of what he should do. He saw Marcel struggling to swim back towards the beach, kicking out hard. He saw Marcel's parents swimming out to reach him, his father shouting something to him or to Marcel; he didn't know, he couldn't hear what it was above the roaring in his ears. And still he dithered. He faced forward again to see where the sea was leading him, too scared to get off the lilo, too terrified. Rocks loomed up in front of him. Frantically he tried to paddle sideways to avoid them, his arms and legs moving with a force he didn't know he possessed. The lilo span and bucked beneath him in the powerful current. He gave up paddling and clung to it, hanging on for dear life. He closed his eyes, willing the lilo to avoid the rocks, wishing this moment could be wiped out. He wanted to be back in safety, inside the line of breakers, playing near the beach. He wished the nightmare would end. But when he opened his eyes there was nothing but a mass of rock ahead. It raced towards him, dark grey and sinister. It was the last thing he saw.

The lilo was tossed against the rock. Thomas's head banged on hard stone.

CHAPTER 13

In the night Julia heard a car, Simba barking once, twice, footsteps. A light went on in the hall. She yawned and turned over, wrapping the sheet more tightly around her.

She floated back to consciousness again. There was someone in her room, standing at her bedside, who bent and kissed her. Recognizing the familiar smell of her mother, she drifted back off to sleep.

In the morning when she sat down to breakfast, Thomas wasn't there. Her mother and father came in. First one hugged her and then the other. She put down her spoon and watched them as they sat down. Something dreadful had happened; she knew it. She could see it in her father's tired, red eyes and the puffiness of her mother's eyelids. Her father, she noticed, had forgotten to brush his hair and it was sticking up like a pineapple top. Her mother picked up her spoon to eat her paw paw but made a small choking sound and put it down again. Her father reached out and covered her hand with his. No one spoke. She could hear sounds of movement in the kitchen and the birds outside, but here there was silence.

At last Julia opened her mouth. 'Where's Thomas?'

she asked. Her voice seemed to be coming from a long way off, it sounded so faint in her ears.

Her father cleared his throat. 'He's in hospital.'

Her eyes flickered to her mother who nodded, returned to her father. 'Hospital?' she asked stupidly. Her mind suddenly sharpened. The greegree man had come for them after all, she thought.

'He's unconscious, darling,' her mother explained.

'Is he dying?'

Her mother began to cry, tears dripping on to the table.

'No,' her father said sharply.

Julia got off her chair and went round to stand at her mother's side. Her mother's arm came up and held her.

'Why is he in hospital?' she asked, dreading what she would hear. From her mother's side of the table she could see The Hill. At this time of the morning it was shrouded in mist. The thick trees made the green of The Hill very dark. Those trees that she had crawled through, she and Thomas. She shuddered.

'He and Marcel were carried out to sea at Grand' Anse,' her father said. 'On a lilo. Bloody idiots!' Julia flinched. She had never heard him speak in such a tense, hard way before. 'Marcel's all right; his father got to him just in time. Thomas was swept up against a rock. Luckily it trapped him. If it hadn't, he would have been drowned. What the hell did they think they were up to!'

Julia's mother gestured weakly at him to calm down.

124

Julia opened her mouth, shut it, opened it again. 'How far did they get?' she asked, wondering sickly if the treasure man might have had anything to do with it too. Maybe Thomas and Marcel had reached him and he'd chased them away, back out to sea.

Her father stared at her. 'How far? Far enough!'

'We've been at the hospital most of the night,' Julia's mother said. 'You were asleep when we left.' Dimly Julia remembered her mother's kiss. 'We're going back there now. Would you like to come with us?'

Julia nodded. And today was the day of her school play, she thought miserably. A finger of mist lifted from The Hill. It seemed to be pointing at her. She turned round so that her back was to the table and she could not see it. She had told Thomas not to go on the lilo, she had known it was dangerous and so had he, why had he done it, why hadn't she stopped him, oh why?

There was no change, the nun said. Thomas was still in a coma and couldn't speak to them. She bustled ahead, the wooden beads of the rosary that hung from her girdle swinging at her side. Julia followed her parents in. A high bed stood in the middle of the small whitewashed room. French windows, hooked back, led out to a verandah. Long white curtains billowed in, almost touching the sheets. Everywhere Julia looked was white, including the bandages round Thomas's head and the tinge of his skin beneath. Another nun was sitting at the bedside. She got up when she saw them and fussed at the sheet, the white of her habit merging into the bedclothes.

'I'll leave you then,' she said, hovering still. 'Just ring the bell if you need me. Or if there's any change,' she added.

Julia's father nodded.

Julia came closer to the bed. 'Hello, Thomas,' she whispered and waited, but he didn't answer. She felt tight and small and scared inside.

They left her mother in the hospital with Thomas, and her father drove her to school in silence. He came with her into the classroom to explain her being late and spoke in a low voice to Sister John while the others looked on curiously. Sister John nodded, her eyes on Julia.

'See you later, poppet,' her father said, hugging her briefly. 'Be good.'

'Daddy –' but he was gone, and half the class was staring at her. She swallowed hard to stop the tears coming. She'd wanted to remind him it was the school play tonight. She thought he might have forgotten. Suddenly it seemed vital that he came to it even though Thomas was in hospital. She felt it was really important that everything should go on as it usually did; she didn't understand why.

She worked hard in geography and arithmetic, trying to lose herself. But in English they were asked to write a composition about adventure at sea, and all she could think of then was Thomas on the lilo, flicking his hair impatiently from his eyes, Thomas sailing away, Thomas struggling in the sea, Thomas being swept up against a rock. Thomas now in darkness. She thought of the greegree man. She thought of candles.

When she got home, she went straight to her bedroom and changed out of her uniform into a dress. She even washed her hands and face before going to find Thérèse.

'Thérèse –'

Thérèse picked up the iron from the kitchen stove, spat on her fingers and touched its base. It sizzled. Satisfied, she carried it back to the table on the verandah where she was doing the ironing before paying attention to Julia.

'Thérèse, do you think the greegree man knows who Thomas is?'

Thérèse put down the iron with a bang. The table shook.

Julia flinched but went on. 'Do you think he knows who I am?'

Thérèse's knuckles were white where she was holding the table. She looked at Julia and said fiercely, 'You are not to talk about him. I've told you that before. You were forbidden to go up The Hill but you went. It's done. Now forget it.'

Julia stared at her dumbly. How could she forget it? Thomas and she had also been forbidden to play on the lilo at Grand' Anse. Somehow she felt the two were linked.

'Did you tell your parents?' Thérèse asked, checking.

She shook her head.

'Good. Because they've got enough to worry about without that.'

Tears came to Julia's eyes.

Thérèse rescued the iron from the sheet that it was beginning to singe and rested it on the stand. 'Now look at what you've made me do.' She caught sight then of Julia's stricken face and bent to her, put her arm round her and her voice softened: 'And I almost forgot to give you a message from your father.'

Julia looked at her hopefully.

'I'm to take you to school at six to get ready for the play and I'll stay to watch. Either your mother or your father will come to see it.'

Julia managed a watery smile.

'*Chérie*, why don't you go for a walk?' Thérèse went on. 'Go and find Cécile. That'll make you feel better. Ask her if she wants to come back and play.'

Julia sniffed. 'She won't be able to. She's always having to look after the kids.'

'Then go there and play,' Thérèse suggested.

'What's the matter with Thomas?'

'He's unconscious.'

'Yes, I know,' she said, fretting. 'But why is he unconscious? Won't he ever speak again?'

'Julia, I don't know. Oh, of course he will. Anyway brooding won't help. Go and find Cécile. The two of you can practise your lines. Go on,' and she gave her a little push.

Julia shuffled her feet. She didn't want to practise anything. She wanted to stay with Thérèse at home.

Then she had an idea. Pierre! That was it. She would go and find Pierre. She would be able to talk to him. He might even be able to tell her what to do.

'All right,' she said to Thérèse, and set off purposefully down the drive, ignoring the suspicious look she'd seen come into Thérèse's eyes at the sudden change in her mood.

Julia went the way she had gone with Thérèse. She passed near Cécile's house. She did look quickly in case Cécile was sitting outside on the steps, but she wasn't. Relieved, Julia carried on down to the market. There was very little traffic about and only a few stalls were still doing business. Four rickshaws were parked at the kerb. She went up to the small group of drivers.

'*Bonjou*.'

'*Bonjou*,' they greeted her back.

'Please, have you seen Pierre?'

'Not since seven this morning,' one of them answered.

'He was outside the cathedral last time I went past,' another said. 'About half an hour ago.'

'Thank you,' and she was off running to the cathedral. At the steps were a few more rickshaws. She went past each in turn but still found no Pierre. She sat on one of the steps, trying to decide where best to wait for him.

The cathedral clock above her clanged out the half hour. She twisted round to see what time it was. She saw the clock for the Devil first: half past six. At half past six it would be dark up on The Hill, she thought.

The real clock said three. Her eyes dropped from it to the open door, a dark rectangle in the white façade at the top of the bright white steps. She got to her feet and climbed them, counting. At twenty she was at the door and breathing in the musty, fragrant smell. She entered the cathedral, passing into the cool, dipping her fingers into the stoup of holy water at the door and making the sign of the cross as you were meant to. Ahead of her, slightly to the side, the candles were burning. Their flickering flames drew her to them. She gazed at them, four rows of candles, half lit, some burnt almost down. One sputtered in a sudden draught. She turned but saw nothing in the shadows. Reassured, she watched them again. Her face glowed from their warmth. She wished she had a coin to drop into the box so that she could take a new one and light it in another's flame and set it straight and tall to burn. For Thomas. She wondered who the money went to. Perhaps it didn't matter. Slowly she stretched out her hand.

A door slammed somewhere in the cathedral.

She spun round and was out and in the hot sunshine and running down the steps, heart thudding.

'Pierre!'

He was just setting down the shafts.

'Hello Julia. Why are you in such a hurry?' He seemed pleased to see her. 'Are you well?'

She nodded and sat down, burying her head in her knees and clasping her ankles in an effort to calm down. Pierre sat down beside her on the step. She heard him shake tobacco on to paper.

'Is your father well?' he went on. Even his questions were familiar. 'And your mother? Your brother?'

'Thomas is in hospital,' she answered finally, turning her head and looking at him sideways. 'They say he's in danger. I think they mean he's dying only they're not telling me.'

Pierre squinted at her. He licked the cigarette paper thoughtfully, put the cigarette in his mouth and lit it.

'Dying?' he asked. 'Why should he die?'

'Because he went on a lilo at Grand' Anse. And we went up The Hill at night, you know, where the greegree man lives.'

Pierre got to his feet abruptly, shaking his head. 'I have to go, Julia. Must look for customers.'

She looked up at him. There was an expression in his eyes that eluded her. 'But Pierre, I wanted to ask you something.' He picked up the shafts of the rickshaw.

In a bound she was standing in the road in front of him, blocking his way.

'What is it?' he asked curtly.

'Do you think the greegree man knows who we are, me and Thomas?'

Pierre's expression didn't change.

Julia waited for him to answer. He didn't.

'I have to know,' she said urgently. 'There's no one else I can ask. Thérèse won't tell me.'

Pierre shifted his hands on the rickshaw shafts.

'Is that why he's unconscious? Does he want us for his candles?' she whispered, desperate.

Pierre heard the fear in her voice.

131

'Listen to me, Julia,' he said at last, 'and listen good. You must not meddle with such things. You mustn't and nor must I. Now hurry home.' He pulled out into the road and began to trot away from her.

She set off home as he had told her. There was nothing else to do. Where the path came out, about half a mile from home, was an old graveyard where French planters were buried. Once she and Thomas and Marcel had explored it. The tombs were above ground. They were of stone and had names and pictures carved on to them. A few had coats-of-arms. Some yawned widely, pushed open by the rampaging tropical flowers and shrubs. Once, when Thomas dared her to, she had put her arm inside, right up to her elbow. When she had told him it was his turn he had laughed and turned away. Now he couldn't even laugh. She looked at the tombs then turned her back on them. They were scary. Large white-washed stones marked the edge of the road. One was flatter than the others. Deliberately she sat on it, her back to the tombs, defying them. Far below her the sea sparkled in the sun. Boats crept out across the water like silent beetles. A schooner, three sails firm in the breeze, made its way to the island of St Anne where dead sharks were dried. A cock crowed back down the path. Small yellow and green birds swooped and peeped around her. Further off she heard the flapping and raucous chatter of a mynah bird. She closed her eyes and concentrated hard on the picture of Thomas in bed in hospital.

She felt something light on her arm and opened her

eyes. A bright green lizard was running up in fits and starts, its tiny feet on her flesh only the merest tickle. It raised its head each time it stopped to see if she was watching. She sat absolutely still, watching its delicate, darting movements. Whenever it stopped, the mighty pulse that kept it alive throbbed in its narrow, fragile neck and shook its whole body. Perhaps the lizard was a sign, she thought.

She would make sure that Thomas did not die. She knew now what to do. The lizard had helped her.

She got to her feet and walked on home, planning.

Branched candlesticks still stood on the dining-room sideboard, filled with new candles, barely burnt. She took one out, found scissors in the drawer and climbed up to her perch in the guava tree. Through the leaves, across the grass, she could see into the kitchen where Noellie and Thérèse were talking; she could hear their voices but not the words. Satisfied that they didn't seem to know she was there, she drew one blade of the scissors down the candle, cutting gently until it split and the wick was exposed, a smooth cord about five inches long. She rolled it into a ball and put it in her pocket, jumped down from the tree, ducked so that Noellie and Thérèse wouldn't see her if they looked out of the window, and fetched a second candle. No one must know what she was doing. Back in the tree she patiently extricated the second wick, rolled it up and put it too in her pocket. She examined the broken candle wax in the lap of her dress, picked it up and smoothed it in her fingers, frowning. The voices had stopped. She looked across into the kitchen. It was empty. She got down from the tree, dug a hole in the soft earth with her hands and buried the broken candles.

There was no one in the pantry when she went in from the dining room. The voices were coming now from the verandah beyond. She opened the fridge door and pushed aside containers till she found what she was looking for: a blue bowl with muslin netting over it. She looked inside; it was full. Satisfied, she pushed it into the far corner. Just then Thérèse came in.

'I'm just getting some pineapple,' she said quickly, taking it out.

Thérèse took it from her. 'I'll cut it for you.' She cut off a slice, peeled it and handed it to Julia. 'When you've eaten it, would you help me feed the chickens? And then you'd better have your meal and we'll go.'

Julia nodded. She followed Thérèse out on to the back verandah and bit hard into the pineapple. Juice dripped down her arms and off her elbow and made dark round spots on the dusty ground.

Julia, Marie and Cécile were to be on stage as heralds for five precious minutes near the beginning of the play, just after the king entered. Later they were to go back twice as townspeople.

Thérèse had left Julia long ago to sit in the auditorium. All the cast were dressed and made up; the play could begin.

Julia could bear the tension no longer. She sneaked

out across the stage needing to look. But before she could reach the crack in the closed curtain to peep through, Sister Dominic had hauled her back. 'Don't!' she said, 'it's unlucky.'

But the nun had understood. She went away and came back a couple of minutes later. 'Your father is here,' she told Julia. 'He's in the front row next to Monsignor the Bishop. All right now?'

Julia nodded in relief. But she was still too nervous to join in the chatter around her.

'Silence!' Sister Dominic commanded. This was the moment they had all been waiting for. The curtains were pulled back and the play began.

Sweating under her thick make-up, Julia stood in the wings waiting. Marie was further down, nearer the back of the stage, and she could see Cécile in the wings opposite.

'. . . to our lands,' she heard the king say on stage. It was their cue. They marched out solemnly, met in the middle, stamped feet in time and faced forward. Julia's heart pounded. So far they had done it without a mistake. She looked for her father, and caught his reassuring smile. She opened her mouth with the others and –

The Bishop was on his feet, looking annoyed. She shut her mouth again. She saw Sister Agatha hurry up to the Bishop and a whispered conversation take place. All eyes were on the pair. Cécile nudged her. 'Do you think we should just carry on?' she whispered.

'I don't know,' Julia whispered back out of the side of her mouth. 'I don't think so.'

The Bishop was sitting down again.

'Let's try now,' Julia muttered. 'I have imp—'

They got no further. Sister Agatha was beckoning them from the wings. They looked uneasily at each other.

Then Sister Dominic was on stage at their side. 'Come off at once, you three!' she hissed.

Julia glanced down at her father. He was looking as upset now as the Bishop. The girls trailed unhappily off stage and the play began again, falteringly, without them.

'The Bishop says you're showing too much of your legs!' Sister Agatha said crossly. She was red and flustered. They didn't know if she was cross at them or at the Bishop. 'He says it's indecent for half your thighs to be showing. But you're meant to be men! Such nons—' At a look from Sister Dominic, she bit back the word. She put an arm round Julia as her face began to quiver. 'Never mind,' she said more quietly. 'Let's go and see if we can find something else for you all to wear for the dancing.'

But the play was spoiled now for Julia. She was glad when her father came backstage at the end and asked if she minded leaving right away.

They got into the car, with Thérèse in the back. She smiled sympathetically at Julia but didn't speak.

'Poor Julia,' her father said. 'What an impossible man that bishop is. Are you very disappointed?'

'No,' she said bravely, shaking her head.

'Good girl.' He patted her knee. 'There are worse things,' he muttered to himself.

She heard him and knew he meant Thomas. His face was set and closed off. She looked away and miserably watched the familiar landmarks flit quickly past till they were at home.

They walked in side by side, his arm loosely around her shoulders. 'Come and sit with me while I eat, before I put you to bed?' he said. 'Then I'm going back to the hospital.'

Julia nodded. Thérèse set a small plateful of food in front of her so that she could keep her father company. Dinner was swift and almost silent. She watched her father shovel in half his food. Once or twice she opened her mouth to speak but thought better of it. He left the other half of his meal. She ate slowly, hoping to delay him.

'Will Mummy come and say good-night later?' she asked, when they had finally left the table and he was tucking her in.

'Of course she will,' he said, kissing her. 'But don't stay awake waiting; we may be late home. Will you be all right?'

She heard the anxiety in his voice and nodded mutely, trying to look as reassuring as she could.

'Well Thérèse is here. Call her if you want her.' He rumpled her hair. 'Good-night,' and he was gone.

She heard the car go down the drive and the sound of the engine die away. Her tummy felt cold and cramped. She wished she hadn't eaten. She almost wished her father hadn't bothered coming to the play. She pushed her head into the pillow and began to cry, great big tears that felt as if they would never stop, weeping out her disappointment. She wished things would go back to the way they had been. If only Thomas would get better. At last she began to calm. Slowly she realized what she had decided to do, sitting at the graveyard. Comforted, at last she fell asleep.

In the night she woke up. She beat out with her arms, knocking off cockroaches that she thought were there, but when she opened her eyes there were no dark blobs on the pale sheet, no monstrous beetles on her skin, nothing there. Only the darkness of the night.

She pulled back her sheet and ran to her parents' room, round to her mother's side. She got in and cuddled up against her.

CHAPTER 14

By the time her parents started on their toast, Julia had finished her breakfast.

'Would you like to come with us this afternoon to see Thomas?' her father asked.

After a pause, she shook her head. He didn't seem to mind.

She spooned sugar into her empty cup, poured some tea over it and watched the ants struggle to the sides. She picked them out with her teaspoon.

'May I go now?' she asked.

'So soon?' Her mother sounded sad. There were puffy bags around her eyes.

Julia mumbled something about wanting to be early at school.

Her mother nodded dully.

Julia turned. On the way to school she turned left to the hospital and went in through the large open doors.

The nun in the hall looked up. 'What are you doing here? You should be at school. There's no visiting, you know, not until this afternoon.'

'School doesn't start till half past eight,' Julia said in a polite voice. 'And, please, I've come to see my brother. I have to tell him something important.' She was edging towards the wide stairs as she spoke.

'Your brother?' the nun queried. 'Oh, you must be the Geddes girl.' She peered at her over her spectacles and her voice softened slightly. 'But your brother is in a coma, dear. He won't be able to hear you.'

A younger nun who had come into the hall as the older one finished speaking, crossed to the desk and talked in a low murmur to her, their heads close together.

Julia took another few steps towards the stairs.

'What's your name?' The clear voice rang out. She stopped guiltily.

'Julia,' she replied.

'Very well, Julia. Sister Agnes has persuaded me to make an exception for you. I don't see why. Rules are rules and we should obey them. However, you may have two minutes with your brother. Sister Agnes will take you up. Sister—'

Sister Agnes held out a hand to Julia who took it thankfully. She relinquished it as soon as they reached the top of the stairs.

'Only two minutes, mind,' Sister Agnes said, opening the door and leading her into the room.

Julia's eyes flew to Thomas. Nothing had changed. He lay just as he had lain on her last visit, still and wan under the bandages. She came closer and touched his hand. She leaned over till her lips were close to his ear, the unbandaged one, and whispered so that the nun couldn't hear, 'Tonight, Thomas. I'm going to go up The Hill again. Tonight. Can you hear me, Thomas? I'll give the greegree man his candle. Are you listening?' She watched him carefully for any sign of a

140

response. 'Tonight,' she repeated again, more loudly. She was convinced that he could hear her. She kissed the tip of his nose and left the room.

'Thank you,' she said to the nun downstairs, who merely grunted, not looking up. She walked resolutely out of the hospital and on to school. There was no turning back now. She was committed.

Four o'clock. Her parents had been at the hospital since lunchtime and were having a break from their vigil at Thomas's bedside. 'Mummy needs some air,' her father explained. She had about an hour, Julia thought, glancing surreptitiously at her father's watch on the wrist that hung at his side. His other hand was holding her mother's. 'Are you sure you wouldn't like to come?' her mother twisted the ends of her tie belt in her fingers as her father spoke.

Julia nodded, very firmly, resisting her parents' appeal. If they went for a walk that would give her an hour. Noellie and Thérèse had gone out and wouldn't be back until sunset. Now was the time.

'Of course I'll be all right,' she reassured her father when he asked.

She waited until her parents had walked down the slope and she could no longer see the yellow of her mother's dress through the bushes, and then she went into the pantry. She took out the blue bowl from the fridge, untied the muslin net around it and examined the lumps of fat inside that Noellie had cut off the half pig they had been sent as a present two weeks before.

She took the bowl through to the kitchen. The cast-iron stove was only giving out a little heat. She opened the fuel door and put in wood from the box at the side as she had seen Noellie do and closed the door again with a clang.

Disturbed by the noise, a cockroach crawled out from the side of the wood box. Julia gave a little scream. She bit her lip hard to control its special twitching. She couldn't let the cockroach stop her now. Bravely she reached out over the insect to the box, pulled out a piece of wood and slammed it down hard on the beast. Dead. With the end of the wood she pushed it under the stove, back into the darkness.

She swallowed hard. She went over to the cupboard, tipped the lumps of fat into a pan, put the lid on it, set it on the stove. Then and only then she allowed herself to look up at the kitchen clock. Ten minutes had gone already. She waited.

She lifted the lid. The fat was beginning to sweat but it didn't seem to be melting.

Then she remembered that she hadn't turned up the dial at the side of the stove to increase the heat. She did so now and waited for five minutes, watching the hand of the kitchen clock. By the time it reached four she heard a definite sizzling which was louder by five. She lifted the lid. It reeked now of fat. About half the lumps were slowly turning to liquid.

She put the lid back on and ran outside, lifted herself up to her bedroom window-sill and landed on her bed the other side. She looked under her T-shirts for the two lengths of cord she had taken from the candles the day before. Her tin of treasures was under her pillow. She picked this up too and went back to the kitchen the way she had come.

She took two small thick glasses from the kitchen cupboard and set them on the side.

Twenty minutes gone.

The fat was melting nicely now, only a few lumps left. She stirred it with a spoon, eyes closed, concentrating hard, trying to ignore the thick sweet smell.

She picked up the pan and carefully tipped liquid fat into each glass.

The lengths of wick were far too long for the glasses. She took Noellie's knife, the one Noellie never allowed her to touch, and quickly cut through the end of the wicks to shorten them.

The sharp knife, coming up, sliced her thumb. She didn't even notice until the blood began to drip.

'Ow,' she said automatically, though it hadn't hurt. She looked at the blood. Of course! It was exactly what she needed. She held her thumb over first one glass then the other, not trying to staunch the flow. Blood spiralled through the liquid fat, her blood. She watched it fall till it began to clot on her thumb. She wiped it off on the wicks. She sniffed the glasses. She didn't think they smelled any more human now that her blood was in them, but she expected that the greegree man would.

The wick wouldn't stay upright in the fat; it was still too liquid. She took the glasses through and put them in the ice compartment of the fridge. Back in the kitchen she opened her tin and shook out her treasures: the dried-up lizard, the cinnamon leaf skeleton, the two teeth and, lastly, her magic bean. She shook out the tiny ivory animals from the bean and divided them into two small piles, one beside the lizard and Thomas's tooth, the other beside the leaf skeleton and hers.

When she had tipped the rest of the contents of the pan back in the bowl she waited another five minutes. Thirty-five minutes gone. Another twenty-five and she had to be finished.

She took out the glasses again. This time the fat was solidifying nicely. She sprinkled the animals into them. Some sank; others remained on the surface. She plopped in the teeth. Finally she added the wick and put them back in the ice compartment. Then she put water on to boil.

She sat on the verandah, fidgeting, keeping an eye out for her parents.

Back in the kitchen she looked at the clock. Only ten minutes left.

To the ice compartment. She prodded the fat. To her relief it was hard. She poured hot water into the pan and dipped the glasses into them. She ran a blunt knife between the glass and candle, once, twice. To her joy, the candles came away.

Five minutes left. Quickly she pressed the cinnamon leaf into the side of one, and the dried lizard into the other.

It had worked! She put the yellowy candles on a plate, covered them reverently with a white linen napkin and hid them carefully in the furthest corner of the fridge behind the tins of jam where, she thought, no one else would see them.

Quickly she returned to the kitchen to clear up, wash up, turn the stove down again, wipe away the traces. Finally she scrubbed her nails clean. She dried her hands and sniffed them. Candles! she thought triumphantly.

A lump of fear came into her throat at what she now had to do. She swallowed hard.

She took her book to the guava tree and waited for her parents to return, trying to read.

Dinner that night was even worse than the previous evening. Julia watched her mother toy with her food. Her father had returned to the hospital after their walk. Julia had watched him drive away, hunched unhappily over the wheel. Her mother was staying with her till bedtime 'to keep you company,' she'd said. They'd tried playing cards but it hadn't been much fun because Julia had kept winning and she knew it was because her mother wasn't really trying.

Then they'd decided to have dinner early. First they had watched the sun set, had stood on the grass by her guava tree looking up at The Hill, waiting for the red ball of fire to drop behind it and turn the sky into a vivid purple and orange spread of flames. When it was dark they had gone in from the verandah and sat at the table. Julia had solemnly lit the candles.

And now her mother was playing with her meat, pushing it from one side of her plate to the other.

Julia ate quietly, watching her furtively through her eyelashes.

Her mother looked up and saw her looking. She stretched out an arm to Julia. Her bangles tinkled as they hit the wood of the table. 'I'm so sorry. I'm not being much company, am I?'

'Yes, you are,' Julia said bravely, trying to cheer her up.

Her mother smiled wanly. 'Have you finished?'

Julia nodded.

'Then come and walk with me.'

They walked round the bungalow in the dark, something they had never done before, round and round. Five times. Julia counted. She didn't like it. 'This is just like being back on ship and going round and round the promenade deck for exercise,' her mother tried to joke. Julia didn't think it was funny.

When bedtime came at last, her mother read her a story, something she had not done for a long time. Julia's eyelids drooped. She was only faintly aware of a light being turned off, of a car coming up the drive, doors slamming and a car driving away again.

Later she heard them return. She made herself wake up properly. She wanted to run for their bed. She couldn't. Not this night. She waited.

CHAPTER 15

Julia pulled back the sheet and got up, almost standing on Simba. He grunted and raised his head to peer at her.

'Stay,' she told him. She didn't want him getting in the way. She opened her door and hesitated, listening to her parents' breathing. She crept to the pantry. She took one candle from the fridge, the one with the lizard and Thomas's tooth, put it and a box of matches into a brown paper bag and set off the way she had gone with Thomas that first night, the way they should not have gone. And this time she was alone.

She went through the bushes beside the drive. She crossed the plain with the palm trees. She did not falter.

She began to climb The Hill, heading for the clearing where they had stopped the first time.

Walk on, she told herself sternly. A branch whipped across her face and she opened her mouth to scream. She closed it quickly. 'Walk on,' she mimed the words to herself. This time there was no choice. This time she could not turn back just because she was scared.

And that thought made her braver. She took another step and another. All she had to do was walk, she told herself, one step at a time. She stifled another scream as she blundered into a thick cobweb that spread across her nose and eyelashes. She clawed the sticky thread off her face and went on, counting her footsteps, concentrating on the counting, pushing down the fear.

There was a dip in the ground she didn't remember from before. She hesitated, unsure of the direction. Something large crawled across her foot. Furry legs tickled the top of her instep. She felt a soft body hump upwards and slither forwards. She looked down and saw a dark shadow. A giant centipede, she guessed, shuddering in horror. She shook it aside before it could bite her and broke out into a run.

Only for a couple of paces. Oh God, she thought, the greegree man'll hear me. But there was nothing, only a deep and suffocating silence, dark shadows all around, pressing in on her.

She took a deep breath and edged forward once more. She was glad she had on her dark blue nightgown and not the paler one as before. This one wouldn't show up so much against the dark of the trees.

One hundred and twenty, she counted, one hundred and twenty-one. Each step led her nearer to the greegree man. One hundred and forty-two. Something crackled in the thick bushes ahead of her. She froze, her scalp crawling.

If he was watching her, her steps would be taking her straight to him.

One hundred and sixty-three. She had to go on. Her throat was dry. Her heart was pounding.

She came to a clearing, one that she didn't recognize. She stood at its edge, still in the undergrowth, looking, searching. The other clearing she'd been aiming for wasn't far away but perhaps, she hoped, this would do instead.

She scanned the bushes on the other side. Nothing moved. No wind, no birds. Not even an ant to crawl over her foot.

Bravely she stepped out on to the grass and into the ominous silence.

She knelt and opened the paper bag, cursing it soundlessly for the rustling it made. She took out the candle and set it up on the grass. It fell over. Sweat broke out on her face and her back. She looked around fearfully at the bushes again.

Nothing.

She tried again. She set the candle on a flatter piece of ground. This time it stayed upright.

The brown paper crackled loudly a second time as she shook out the matches.

She lit one. She cupped the flame in her hand though there was no breeze. She brought it to the wick of the candle.

The flame moved slowly down the wick.

She must not stir until the candle itself began to burn, must not, must not. She pinched herself to still her trembling. She no longer dared look up. She concentrated on the candle. 'Burn,' she said, moving her lips though no sound came out. 'Burn,' and it began to.

The flame reached the fat of the candle. Slowly it

began to melt. Thin black smoke rose straight up into the air. Burning fat intruded among the smells of dark earth and grass and rotting vegetation. Animal fat. Her blood, her candle, her sacrifice.

She closed her eyes and summoned up Thomas in hospital, Thomas all in white, the curtains billowing into the room, moonlight across the floor. Thomas pale in the moonlight.

'Thomas,' she whispered, and her whisper made the black smoke dance a little in the air. 'Thomas, get better. Let him get better,' she begged. The end of her lizard skeleton, embedded in the wax, caught fire in a flash of light which then subsided again. Still the black smoke plumed upwards. She gritted her teeth and waited, waited for more candle to burn, hoping that the greegree man would not come to find the smell, not yet, not just yet, not until she had left the clearing, not till she was off The Hill.

'Julia?' Thérèse stopped at the door to the dining room, surprised to see Julia there so early.

'Please may I have breakfast now?' Julia asked as she sat down, all ready in her school uniform.

'Aren't you going to wait for your parents?' Thérèse asked.

Julia shook her head.

'I don't know what's got into you,' Thérèse grumbled, putting grapefruit in front of her. 'This is the second time running you've been early for breakfast. You're up to something. I know you. And you look dreadful,' she added. 'Are you feeling all right?'

She came over and felt Julia's forehead. Julia gazed demurely down at her grapefruit and forced a segment into her mouth. Her other hand pulled her tunic down over her knees in case there were any more scratches there. Her legs were aching with tension and excitement.

'I'll just have bread, please,' she said, stopping Thérèse toasting it. She spread it with guava jam and took a bite but found she didn't want it, her stomach was so tense and hard.

She put it down on her plate and pushed it a little to one side.

'Go on. Finish it,' Thérèse told her.

'I'm not hungry,' she muttered.

'It's as well for you that Thomas is in hospital or you wouldn't get away with this,' Thérèse said crossly.

Julia bit her lip.

'Oh, Julia, I'm sorry.' Thérèse looked stricken. 'Go on then. Go wherever it is you want to go. I'll let your parents know you've gone,' she said in exasperation, leaving the room.

As Julia rounded the table she risked a glance up at The Hill. She didn't know what she expected to see. It looked just the same as on every morning: dark, misty and mysterious. Nothing seemed to have changed. She closed her eyes, opened them and looked again. Still nothing.

She went to the fridge to take out the second candle. Thérèse, coming in, stared to see Julia putting it in a paper bag, but Julia was out and running down the drive before she could stop her, and when she called out, 'Where are you going with that?' she thought she must have imagined the faint answer back: 'To the cathedral.'

Julia half ran, half walked the way to school, keeping to the shade as much as she could, holding the paper bag gingerly by finger and thumb so that the candle didn't touch her warmth or that of the sun. She didn't want it to melt.

When she reached the cathedral, people were coming out of early mass alone and in small groups, the women in their floral dresses fanning themselves with their hats. They looked curiously at the small fair-haired girl in her school uniform waiting politely at the door for them to pass, but no one said anything. Julia waited for the last one to leave then slipped inside. She hesitated until her eyes had become accustomed to the relative gloom, then walked towards the bank of candles. She took the cinnamon-leaf candle out of the paper bag and put it down among the others, resting it on top of a holder because it was too wide to fit into it. It stayed there, balanced, far more yellow than the others around. Satisfied, she picked it up and tipped the wick into the flame of the neighbouring candle. It sputtered, spat and took. She set it upright on the holder again, wiped the fat off her hands and on to her legs and waited. Down the wick came the flame. It reached the top of the fat and began to smoke blackly, releasing its pungent smell.

She dropped to her knees. 'Our Father –' she began but went no further. It was the wrong prayer for now. Again she concentrated on Thomas in his hospital bed. 'Dear God, have mercy on his soul,' she said aloud as the tip of the leaf skeleton caught fire. She couldn't think what else to say so she repeated the words over and over again with mounting urgency, 'Have mercy on his soul, mercy on his soul, mercy. Amen.'

Her mind went a blank.

She got to her feet. She began to walk away, out of the cathedral, very slowly, her eyes not leaving the candle for a moment. One step, another. The floor of the cathedral seemed huge, the space she had to cover vast. 'Mercy,' she whispered as she took another step, 'on his soul.' She didn't allow herself to turn, not until she had backed out of the door and was standing in the sunshine once more.

Lessons were beginning, geography and maps and drawing – and Sister John looked up in the middle of a sentence.

Julia's father was in the doorway of the class. Julia froze. He walked down the row of desks at the side, not looking at her. His face gave nothing away.

He went to Sister John and whispered.

Sister John's face broke into a wide smile.

'Julia,' she called, beckoning.

Julia pushed back her chair. Her ruler clattered to the floor. She picked it up and put it carefully back on the desk. It suddenly seemed very important that she should do so. Her knees were trembling. Her father met her halfway to the teacher's desk. 'Thomas is going to be all right,' he said. 'He's out of his coma. He can speak.' He looked at her in amazement. 'Don't cry, poppet.'

'I can't help it,' she sobbed.

It had worked! Her candles had saved Thomas!

'We'll go and see him again this evening, all right? He's sleeping now. Sister John agrees you may have today off to celebrate.'

Outside on the dusty playground she let her father hold her hand. 'Mummy's waiting in the car. Would you like to do something special today?'

'Let's just go home,' she said.

After lunch her parents lounged in cane chairs on the verandah, celebrating with wine. Julia was on the step, cross-legged, Coke in hand, leaning against her father's legs. She half-closed her eyes and listened happily to them talk, lulled by their voices which were relaxed again as they had not been for days.

'The monsoon's breaking,' her father said suddenly. Julia opened her eyes fully and looked. A dark blanket of rain was sweeping across the sea towards the island. It touched the town below, blotting out the sea and the pier, the playing fields, the asbestos and tin and palm roofs of the capital and now the tops of the trees.

Her father's legs moved. She turned round. Her parents were getting up, holding hands.

'We're going for a siesta,' her mother said. 'See you soon, darling. You'll be all right, won't you?'

Julia nodded, eyes shining, quite happy to be on her own again now. She looked back at the cloud. Now it reached their house and covered it. Its drum cadences descended and thundered out on the corrugated roof above her, silencing the birds. There was nothing to be heard but the mighty pounding. The water seduced her off the verandah and on to the grass. She wrenched her dress off over her head and threw it aside. She lifted her face to the tumult and within seconds her short hair was streaming. She spread her arms wide and danced about the sodden grass, now a sheet of grey water. The rain poured over the full gutters and she stood beneath to catch the waterfall on her shoulders. The water raced down the verandah steps and she put her feet below the bottom one to feel it push through her toes. She threw herself on her back into the shallow lake of grass, laughing for joy and wonder.

Abruptly the rain stopped. There was a moment's surprised silence. Then the birds resumed their raucous chatter. Raising herself on one elbow on the wet grass, Julia watched the rain move away across the valley and the steam rise in a misty cloud as the sun beat down.